The Secret of
Ventriloquism
Jon Padgett

DUNHAMS MANOR PRESS
East Brunswick, New Jersey

Published by

DUNHAMS MANOR PRESS
C/O
DYNATOX MINISTRIES
East Brunswick, New Jersey
USA

www.dunhamsmanor.com
www.dynatoxministries.com

for Carolyn, Mamie, and Tom

Contents

Introduction

S. T. Joshi has famously argued that the truly great authors of weird fiction have been great precisely because they use their stories as a vehicle for expressing a coherent worldview. I would here like to advance an alternative thesis. I would like to assert that one of the characteristics of great weird fiction, and most especially weird horror—not the sole characteristic, of course, since weird horror is a multifaceted jewel, but a characteristic that is crucial and irreducible in those works of the weird that lodge in the reader's mind with unforgettable force and intensity—is a vivid and distinct authorial *voice*.

Can you imagine Poe's "The Fall of the House of Usher" without the sonorous narrative voice that speaks from the very first page in tones of absolute gloom and abject dread? Can you imagine Lovecraft's "The Music of Erich Zann" minus its voice of detached, dreamlike trepidation tinged with cosmic horror, as generated by the author's distinctive deployment of diction and artistry of prose style? Or Shirley Jackson's *The Haunting of Hill House* without the striking establishment of voice in the classic opening paragraph ("No live organism can continue for long to exist sanely under conditions of absolute reality; even larks and katydids are supposed, by some, to dream…"), which then develops over the course of the novel into a sustained tone of mingled dread, loneliness, and melancholy? Or what about Ligotti's "The Last Feast of Harlequin" without its measured tone of fearful discovery foregrounded against an emotional backdrop of desolate inner wintriness, as delivered in the narrative voice of an unnamed social anthropologist investigating a strange clown festival in an American Midwestern town? Each of these stories would be not just diminished but fundamentally altered—neutered, hamstrung, eviscerated—by the removal of its distinctive voice, which, vitally, is not just the narrative voice of the individual story but the voice of the author expressing itself through the environment of that particular work.

The point is not, of course, that these writers always maintain the very same voice in multiple works. Poe creates many different narrative voices across the span of his complete oeuvre. But he always, on some level, sounds like Poe. The same is true of Lovecraft, Jackson, Ligotti, and the other great masters of weird and supernatural horror. Their voice is vital to their authorial selves. They don't write in the style-less monotone of much commercial horror fiction. In their works you can hear *them* talking in and through the multitude of voices that make up their respective fictional worlds. It's a special kind of literary art, this creation of a distinctive voice that speaks to the reader in unmistakable tones with a manifest force and singularity of identity.

And it is an art that Jon Padgett possesses in spades. I learned this over a span of years as I was privileged to observe, intermittently and from a distance, the germination and gestation of Jon's authorial self. Eventually he started sending stories that fairly stunned me with the force of their philosophical-emotional impact. I remember first being affected like this by "20 Simple Steps to Ventriloquism," in which—significantly—the narrative itself focuses directly on the nature and power of voice, and of one special, dreadful voice in particular, an "intangible, alien voice twisting through that throat and that mouth, telling us that you have only ever been one of its myriad, crimson arms... Feel that voice that is not a voice bubbling through that mouth that is not a mouth. Let it purge you of your static. Let it fill you with its own static." Presented in the form of a step-by-step guide to learning "Greater Ventriloquism"—whose practitioners are "acolytes of the Ultimate Ventriloquist ... catatonics, emptied of illusions of selfhood and identity ... perfect receivers and transmitters of nothing with nothing to stifle the voice of our perfect suffering"—this is one of the most powerful, unsettling, disturbing, and impactful stories of its kind, or really of any kind, that I have read in the last ten years.

The same current of power winds its way through the other works gathered together here. In these nine striking stories—or, more accurately, seven stories plus a one-act play and a guided meditation on experiencing the horror of conscious existence—Jon modulates the voice of his author's self into multiple tones depending on the needs of the piece at hand. In "Organ Void" and "The Infusorium," for example, he calibrates it with galling effectiveness to generate a tone, mood, and worldview of visceral filthiness set in a fictional realm of mounting, horrifying darkness. In

"Murmurs of a Voice Foreknown" he applies it successfully to the first-person depiction of the narrator's personal nightmare of childhood persecution, and the inner transition that leads this young protagonist to realize his power to outdo his persecutor. In "The Mindfulness of Horror Practice" (the aforementioned guided meditation), he sounds almost like one of his non-horror influences, the contemporary spiritual writer and teacher Eckhart Tolle, who speaks unfailingly in a gentle voice of detached lucidity and focused self-inquiry—and yet Jon makes this so much his own that the voice guiding the reader toward a state of liberation from, or rather within, the horrors of body, mind, and being itself is recognizable as perhaps the quintessence of the other narrative voices in the book. In all of this, one can, I think, detect traces of his longtime practice of ventriloquism, as he projects his author's voice into each work and makes it speak convincingly through them all, even as it remains, in essence, his own.

I hope and believe that this, the first full-length book by Jon Padgett, will be remembered as an authentically significant debut collection. Along with voice, it also has vision, as may be evident from the lines I have quoted, and Jon's rich elaboration of this vision goes a considerable distance toward establishing a coherent worldview and thus fulfilling the Joshian criterion. "We Greater Ventriloquists are acolytes of the Ultimate Ventriloquist," announces one of his narrators at the end of twenty transformative lessons. "We Greater Ventriloquists are catatonics, emptied of illusions of selfhood and identity... . We are active as nature moves us to be: perfect receivers and transmitters of nothing with nothing to stifle the voice of our perfect suffering. Yes, we Greater Ventriloquists speak with the voice of nature making itself suffer." I don't know for sure if "the voice of nature making itself suffer" is actually, ultimately, Jon's own voice. For his sake, I think I hope it isn't. But I do know that it is a voice that lodges in the reader's mind with colossal force and intensity, marking that story and this book as unforgettable.

Matt Cardin
Stephenville, Texas
September 2016

When forced to speak, matter *suffers*. The voice that is squeezed out through the dead materials of the mechanism becomes the voice of the mechanism's protest against animation, the voice of its resistance to voice.

-Steven Connor,
Dumbstruck: A Cultural History of Ventriloquism

The Mindfulness of Horror Practice

In this recording I'm going to be leading you through all four stages of the mindfulness of horror practice.

Closing your eyes. Now become aware of your environment—the air on your skin, the temperature in the room, any itches or irritations you might feel, any aches or pains within or without. And acknowledge the sounds around you—cars honking outside, the neighbor's music playing, the screeches of birds or children. Any smells, perfumes or bodily odors. Just become open to these sensations and experiences—accept them, good or bad.

And then you can begin to take your attention inwards into your body. Becoming aware of your feet. Feeling the skin and veins, muscles and sinews, and finally the skeletal structure of your feet. The dead bones of your future self. Feel them becoming more solid than the transitory flesh-gore that covers them. And the more awareness you can take into your skeleton feet, the more you can let go. Now let that sensation spread from your skeleton feet up to your calf bones, thigh bones, pelvic bones, straight up through your spine (poised and balanced), shoulder blades, flexing ribs and collar bones, the bones growing heavy, heavy down your arms, elbows, straight through the tiniest finger bones. Letting the top of your spine grow long, long. Noticing that your skull is the only part of your skeleton that feels light—as if the rest of your head (hair, skin, eyes, cartilage, brain) has disintegrated, leaving a dome filled only with the gaseous remnants of your non-skeletal-self.

And then begin to experience your skeleton as a whole—scanning through it, upright and open. And in the midst of all these experiences, notice a deep aching within your skeleton-self—a throbbing hurt. Concentrate on that skeleton-ache; let it expand within its marrow. Become absorbed, become fascinated by the wellspring of discomfort you've discovered within yourself.

This is the horror of the Organism.

And in the midst of all these experiences, notice your breathing, the physical sensations of your breathing. And you can let your awareness become absorbed, become fascinated by those sensations. Letting your consciousness fill your breathing. And letting your breathing fill your consciousness.

And then moving into the second stage of the practice, noticing your breath—counting one, breathing in and out. Two, in and out. Three, in and out. And so on until you get to ten. And once you've reached ten, starting again at one. And whenever you realize that your mind has wandered, bring your awareness back into your breathing. Noticing the awareness becoming aware of itself and, with it, a growing panic traveling through your body all the way up into your skull every time you breathe in. So every time that you breathe in, your mind is becoming more and more at one with panic, until every counted number becomes a testament to self-suffocation.

This is the horror of the Mind.

And then moving into the third stage of the practice, you can let go of the counting and simply follow the flow of your panicked breathing. As you continue to breathe in and out, beginning to focus on your panicked thoughts. Notice how they flail against the growing agony of the becoming within you. Your panic helping you to stay in awareness, becoming that awareness. Now imagine your every inhaled breath drawing Black Fog in—a killing toxin that exterminates those stray, redundant cogitations that writhe and jerk within the emptying hull of your mind.

This is the horror of Being.

And now moving into the last stage of the practice, you can finally stop breathing altogether and begin focusing more and more on less and less. You may begin to imagine you hear something like static or even the roar of an airliner. You may feel lightheaded like you're going to pass out. Ignore these feelings. They are normal. They indicate that you're coming into perfect sync with your empty skeleton body and your empty skeleton head.

Giving yourself a few moments to assimilate the effects of the practice. And you can begin to take your awareness into the outside world. Becoming aware of the space around you. And of your experiences of that space. As hideous and alien without as within.

Accept as the days and nights go by that you are a walking skeleton, an ambulatory miracle of meat. New thoughts come, but they arrive from beyond the foam, beyond the foam, beyond the foamy sponge of your brain.

Now open your eyes.

Murmurs of a Voice Foreknown

I was seven years old the first time my brother tried to kill me.

"Sam wants you dead," he whispered in my ear one day at our grandmother's house. My brother had received a pellet gun—a Crosman 760 Powermaster—for his twelfth birthday. Soon after our arrival, I watched him fire the new weapon upon the rusted tin-roofed boat dock and wood pilings that lined our grandmother's expansive backyard and the filthy canal beyond it.

"That was you," he would say after each pellet hit its mark with a ping. My brother took aim from various positions around the yard as he fired the rifle. He sprinted and leaped over circles of crab grass and pine straw, ripping the bark off small trees as he wheeled around them.

Unlike my brother, I was neither athletic nor interested in athletics of any kind. Instead, I spent many of those summer days capturing honeybees. I'd trap them and a variety of other insects in an empty juice bottle—its thin, golden metal top riddled with air holes I fashioned with a long-handled ice pick.

When my brother became distracted enough by his target practice, I crept off and retrieved my insect jar and spent the rest of the day capturing bugs, gazing through warped glass at them. My thin-legged inmates—bee, spider and ant—encountered one another there, sometimes more or less peacefully, sometimes with brutal but mesmerizing results.

At the end of the visit, I followed my brother to the car. He was pumping his Crosman again and again, perhaps five feet in front of me. My brother stopped all at once and turned around, aiming his gun's black proboscis at my head.

"Sam says shoot out your eye."

Then he pulled the trigger.

If I hadn't covered my face with my hands, the pellet would have found its mark, causing permanent eye damage or worse. At the time, I was sure it would've killed me on the spot. I'm sure my brother hoped it would. Instead, the miniature bullet struck my right hand's middle fingernail, which exploded into bloody fragments. I looked down at the alien, red nub of my nail-less finger, my mouth open in a long howl of astonished disbelief.

Mother meted out big brother's punishment in short order. He received a long spanking on the spot via The Brush (always on-hand), administered by my diminutive mother while the rest of the family—my father, my grandmother and I—watched on. As usual, my brother chortled through The Brush's every whack, grinning at me as if imagining his pain transmuted into the many torments he would soon inflict upon my body and mind.

I was the younger of two children. Aside perhaps from my sullen father, no one wanted a new addition to the family less than my brother.

I received more injuries and humiliations from him than I can recall during my early childhood. Once he nudged me off the back of his speeding bicycle—which led to a chin full of stitches. Other times I remember him slamming my hand in the car door, hurling me into the sticker bushes in our front yard, even shoving me backwards into the wood piling-lined, rainbow-sheened canal behind our grandmother's backyard. But until his twelfth birthday, he never mentioned anyone named Sam.

"Who's Sam?" I asked my brother one night soon after the pellet gun incident. We were both almost ready for bed, and he had just entered my room.

He sidled up to me, smirking, his breath stinking of hardboiled eggs. Then he put on "the spooky voice"—one to which I had grown accustomed. Each night my brother filled my head with stories, sometimes about the bodiless Hand that lived under my bed. The Hand, crawling about on thin but powerful fingers, waiting for the ideal time to strangle me in my sleep. And then there was the grinning, living Doll who lived in an old trunk up in the attic just down the hall from my bedroom door. The Doll, whose sharp teeth were coated with an incurable poison.

After I asked about Sam, my brother began his spooky-voiced story, as he often did, with one large knuckle jabbed hard into my shoulder. I withstood the pain and tried not to whimper, which I knew would only make the bedtime torment worse.

"Before you were born, pad-butt, mom and dad had another baby. His name was Sam. But little Sam died when he was just tiny. Mom and dad told me they were gonna have another baby, but it turned out to be *a bad mistake*. And that's just what dad said to mom. *A bad mistake*. You were no Sam, and they knew it."

My brother's smirk twisted into a sneer and his voice became a whisper in my ear as he pinched the back of my neck... hard.

"Sam talks to me at night, twig. He tells me it's almost time for you to be dead. And once you die, Sam's gonna take over your body. You'll be gone, but *he'll* be back. I might just kill you for him just to speed things up. I haven't made up my mind yet. You tell mom and dad anything about this, though, and you bet I *will* kill you. Dead."

My brother left me trying not to blubber in my bed with a new demon to torment my sleep—Sam. What would it feel like for something *other* to invade my body and push me out of it? Would I see my own face grinning up with hilarity and malice as I just floated away and disappeared? I doubted whether the Hand or the Doll existed (at least during the day), but I was certain that the malignant shade of Sam *was* real. Hadn't my brother actually tried to kill me? Hadn't my parents both been sad and angry over something unstated for as long as I could remember?

In the months that followed, my brother mentioned Sam every night.

"Sam says stab you in the brain with the ice pick."

"Sam says hold you under the water in the bathtub."

"Sam says smother you with your pillow."

"Sam says almost time."

"Sam says won't be long."

My brother whispered such things to me at the breakfast table, in the kitchen, in my bedroom, in the den, in the front and backyards. Once he even convinced me that Sam spookily entered a statue of a certain cherubic, laughing Buddha. It sat in an attitude of eternal, uncanny glee on my parents' cluttered dresser.

"Now, big-head-little-body," my brother whispered. "You bust that statue, and you're saved."

So I snuck the heavy Buddha figure outside that afternoon and dashed it against the sidewalk in front of our house. Just then, my brother appeared at the open front door with our mother, pointing at me next to the shards of ruined statue. Soon I was receiving the Brush treatment. I sobbed, bent over a chair in the dining room, as my brother danced and silently taunted me out of mother's sight, through the doorway.

After that, I worked harder to avoid being alone with him. I spent as much time as I could outside elsewhere in the neighborhood, searching for bugs to capture. The insects' tiny lives proved a welcome distraction, a kind of temporary bulwark against my brother's shenanigans. Some days passed without incident.

One morning, though, I was washing my hands in the upstairs bathroom when my brother entered behind me and closed and locked the door. He stank of chlorine from a swimming competition the night before. My parents were out of hearing or out of the house altogether. Before I could bolt, my brother placed me in a one-armed chokehold and forced me to look at myself in the mirror.

"This is poison," he said as he held out a handful of bright red pills. At that, he overpowered me and pushed every one of the pills into my mouth.

"Look," he said, pointing at my image in the mirror. "You're dying."

Sure enough, red foam was pouring out of my mouth and down my face.

The scary looking pills turned out to be only harmless, dental disclosing tablets used to reveal plaque on teeth. But through my brother's laughter and my own high-pitched, terrified wailing, I made the decision to take action against further torments.

The night after the dental pill murder fake out, I sat up in the darkness of my bedroom and considered my options. What could I do to defend myself from further psychological and physical damage (or death)?

I heard a slow moving rice beetle buzzing, plinking against my window screen. It made me think about the insects and arachnids and grubs from the flowering hedges or underneath garden bricks or logs or within webs or nests in our carport and backyard. The kind of creatures I collected in my jar—the little crawling and flying things I observed and released, alive or dead. Honeybees, flies, centipedes, inchworms, spiders. I lacked the natural resources that most of these creatures had. I couldn't protect myself like the roly-poly, curling up in its protective shell when assaulted. I lacked the wasp's sting or the spider's nimble web spinning. I was slow as the rice beetle plinking against my bedroom window screen, but I lacked its ability to fly.

A thought occurred unbidden to me: *maybe I am like a daddy longlegs.* Yes, the spiders that my father once told me are not spiders—the ones that spin no webs but amble about on segmented, needle-thin limbs. Legs that break off so easily when grabbed, never to grow back. The non-spider-things that release a terrible, acrid, chemical stench when threatened. That pungent smell was unforgettable.

I remembered my brother once telling me that the small body and tiny head atop the gangling legs of the daddy longlegs had no sting or bite that could pierce human skin. But (and he said this with relish) the daddy-long legs' poison was more venomous than that of any other spider, even if it was unusable—lacking an effective delivery mechanism. I later discovered that my brother was half wrong about the daddy longlegs (or Pholcidae). Its fangs are indeed miniscule, but its venom is far from potent. As far as I knew at the time, though, the gangly insect's poison could kill.

Like the daddy longlegs, I thought, I was clumsy, slow, skinny, harmless. But was there not hidden, potent toxin within me? And—if so—how could I *access* that poison and use it to protect myself against my brother's attacks—or even use it to end his life before he ended mine?

That night, following my brother's spooky-voiced bedtime story —Sam as usual persuading him to kill me in a variety of more or less creative ways—I sat in the gloom of my bedroom, counting to one thousand. My thoughts drifted to the Hand under my bed. Each number I recited seemed punctuated by noiseless fingers crawling up the foot of my bed, inching nearer and nearer. What if the Hand under my bed was *Sam's* hand, growing even after the death of the rest of his infant-body? I forced those thoughts away and shifted my attention back to an idea that began uncurling itself like a roly-poly within my head. My brother, so powerful and malignant during the day, would be helpless in sleep.

Once I finished counting and the house grew quiet, I stood up and tiptoed through the open door towards my brother's bedroom, out into the hallway. As I approached his door, my wary eyes kept watch upon the ceiling attic entrance in which my brother told me so many times the Doll lurked. Past that entrance, in the dark, I could go no further, paralyzed by whirring thoughts of the Doll and her sharp, poisonous teeth. What if the Doll and Sam were now one and the same, another demon-brother clothed in that hideous figure? Would my death by poisonous bite be a prelude to undead possession? I slunk back to my bed and spent another night wracked with fear. All of my brother's monsters—real or imagined—melded together with jagged, segmented limbs and toxic stingers.

The nightmare images lingered into the next day but became divorced from the previous evening's fear. It was as if the mechanism propelling the night horror shorted itself out, leaving only the remaining nightmare-trappings behind, racing back and forth behind my eyes. And behind those nightmare after-images? My brother's hateful face—dark brown eyes shining.

Then I remembered the long-handled ice pick and retrieved it from the kitchen drawer. With that weapon I might stand a chance against Sam-Hand, Sam-Doll, Sam-Buddha, Sam-Sam, my brother, whatever else might attack me in the darkness.

That night, again, I counted to one thousand. Again, I imagined clutching Sam-Hand and grinning Sam-Doll waiting to spring on me. But now I was brandishing the long-handled ice pick. The counting done, I slid out of bed, holding the ice pick in front of me like a flashlight. At the far end of the hall, my brother's room stood, door ajar. I made it past the attic ceiling-door above and slipped inside his bedroom. I imagined myself insubstantial, invisible in the quiet night.

I crept inside and looked around, anticipating ambush. But only my sleeping brother was revealed, half covered by a thin blue blanket, mouth agape. Like a dead fish.

I took in a deep breath and descended to the ground until my torso, arms, and legs were flat on the dusty hardwood floor. Like a daddy longlegs, like the Hand, I crawled under my brother's bed and flipped over onto my back when I was more or less in the same position as my sleeping brother above. I considered the floor, my rail thin limbs and torso and large head upon the floor, box-spring inches above my face, mattress upon box-spring, and my brother upon that mattress, oblivious. And above him, the ceiling with its globular, extinguished light. And beyond that, the attic. And beyond that? And beyond that? My mind emptied of further thought.

I placed the point of the long-handled ice pick on the slatted box-spring below the covered mattress. The bottom of the box-spring was covered with a kind of thin, rough fabric, almost like burlap. I ran the ice pick along it, listening to the soft zipping sound it made. From underneath the bed, I adjusted my position, guessing where my brother's head might be up there. I closed my eyes and envisioned myself floating just above instead of below him, pressing the pointed metal of the pick onto my brother's soft, yielding eyelid. I pushed up against the box-spring and applied just a little more force... and then a little more. *Thwip.* The pick (my stinger) entered the box-spring—big brother's eye and brain in my imagination—within it to the hilt. I realized then that the box-spring was empty—just a hollow frame with rough material stapled around it. I lay underneath the bed in a kind of euphoric glee for the longest time, musing over that emptiness and what could be used to fill it. I was holding the ice pick within the box-spring under my brother's head, my mind clear of fear for the first time in memory. "That was you," I whispered to the prone shape above me.

I spent the next day pacing up and down the length of the flowering hedges in the backyard, collecting honeybees in my jar. And one, then two daddy longlegs, both discovered in a bush covered, pine-straw matted hollow between our house and our neighbor's.

For his part, my brother continued his habitual menace of me, but now his threats seemed as hollow as a box-spring, and his typical swagger felt strained—put on.

"Sam says stick you in the fridge tonight and hold the door closed till you die," he said. I giggled in response.

"You even know how long it'd take for me to run out of air in the refrigerator?" I asked. "How long you'd have to hold it closed? God, you're stupid."

My response surprised both of us. In retaliation he stuck a knuckle into my shoulder and squeezed the nail-less, pink flesh of my injured finger. He twisted it until I shrieked and tears began to run. Until he made me whine for mercy, as I always did. My brother sneered with satisfaction, leaning close to me.

"I've made up my mind, diaper dick. Sam's coming. And you'll be dead soon."

But I knew it was my brother, not me, whose time was drawing to a close.

That night, according to the next phase of my plan, I brought along—in a small canvas bag—the long-handled ice pick, some duct tape and a jar containing the seven bees and two daddy longlegs collected earlier that day. Again I counted to one thousand and crossed my dark bedroom and hall, less fearful than ever of the Hand, the Doll, let alone Sam. Over the past two nights, I had become *one* of them, hidden away in darkness like the Doll, even lurking under a bed like the Hand. And as for the malignant shade of Sam—his obsession with being rehoused in my dead body? Well, that wasn't going to be a problem much longer.

Again I slipped under my brother's bed with my equipment in tow. I inserted the ice pick into the eye-level hole I had created in the box-spring the night before. I twisted the pick around and around, widening the aperture until it was half as big as a quarter.

Twisting off the gold cap, I placed the jar's mouth against the hole. I could smell the daddy longlegs' chemical-protective-fear-stench that had been bottled up for hours. I gagged a little. It struck me that the bees wouldn't exit the jar and enter the box-spring, too drunk on the foul odor. But I was patient. I concentrated on making those buzzing shapes move. One entered the dark cavern above them, whether from the force of my silent concentration or simply to escape the acrid confines of the jar. Then another crawled into the box-spring. Then another.

When all the bees had entered the hollow space, I pressed layer after layer of heavy tape upon the aperture, trapping the insects inside. Afterwards, in the semi-darkness, I listened to the almost imperceptible, erratic hum of bees within my brother's box-spring. Then I set my ear against the rough fabric and listened to the buzzing. I imagined my brother's head melting down, down into the mattress and the box-spring below that, watching in my mind's eye as seven bees crawled one by one into his open mouth.

I scooted out from under the bed and sat cross-legged beside it, now unconcerned that my brother might awaken. I jiggled my insect jar upside-down until the two daddy longlegs fell out onto my small palm. They were both worse for the wear. Two disembodied limbs, one still twitching, fell along with the bugs, and both daddy longlegs were trying without success to raise their small bodies upon needle thin legs that would no longer support any amount of weight. They survived hours of honeybee abuse, and now a nameless giant held them in its hands for a monstrous purpose. I closed my palm into a quivering fist, feeling the spasmodic jerks of daddy longlegs-limbs and the two pea-like bodies popping. The foul stench was almost unbearable now. I stood up, holding my shaking little fist over my brother's prone head, letting several drops of the daddy longlegs fluid drip into his open mouth and finally tossing the remains of the un-spiders under the bed as my brother gagged and coughed, sitting up.

I collected my things and walked backwards, almost gliding, out of his room, unconcerned now whether he saw me or not. My brother hadn't, though—he was still retching. I had never felt emptier or more carefree. And I slept deeply for the rest of the night, unmolested by dreams.

The next morning, my brother was sick in bed, complaining of a bad night's sleep, a sore throat, a buzzing in his ears and a terrible taste in his mouth. I couldn't contain my glee when my diminutive mother told me about it. She scolded me for my giggling grin. But she didn't understand. I knew there was so much more to come. No one knew I had become more cunning than the Hand, more poisonous than the Doll. More secret than Sam.

Later that morning, the first of a new childhood, I ate my colorful cereal, walked up the stairs, and paid my ailing brother a visit. His usually well-tanned skin appeared pale and wet as he sat up in bed. I watched him shaking his confused head, twisting an index finger inside his right ear. The daddy longlegs stench still hung in the air.

"You look bad," I said, ambling up to his bed, sniffing. "And you smell bad too. Maybe Sam decided you'd make a better home for him than I would."

But my brother didn't reach over and stick a knuckle into my scrawny shoulder or twist my injured finger this time. He only averted his shifting, dull brown eyes from my unblinking, eager ones.

"Bro, look," my brother said. "Sam isn't real. I mean, I won't kill you. I wouldn't ever really kill you."

"I know. I know you won't kill me, bro. But one day I'm going to kill *you*."

And one day I did.

The Indoor Swamp

You'll never see any Indoor Swamp employees. No informational tour monologue—not even a recorded voice-over while you ride. The flat-bottomed boat contains no hatch for a driver. A track pulley somewhere under the deck yanks the boat at intervals. You'll feel the automatic pull then release, pull then release of a state fair ride.

The water appears algae-covered green—but not quite the right shade of green. The trees, though, seem realistic. Grayish-white cypresses draped in what looks at first glance like Spanish moss. Some days, an acrid fog hangs over the Indoor Swamp—more mildew than swamp stench.

There is only one Indoor Swamp rule—an off-white sign in front of the dock that reads "NO TOUCHING." This commandment is a little trickier to follow than you'd think. Pay close attention at all times to avoid the hanging branches of burlap-Spanish moss. The closer those trees come as you make your automatic way downstream, the more the bark looks like swaths of dirty papier-mâché. Stroking the jagged, leafless branches as they go by is tempting, just to verify or debunk the trees' natural reality. But you shouldn't.

Of course, it's unclear exactly what the dock-sign means by "NO TOUCHING." Does it mean no touching the off-green liquid, which passes as swamp water? No touching the looming, possibly synthetic trees? The sign offers no elaboration. To be safe, you may want to avoid your fellow passengers—not even touching them with your direct gaze. After all, they'll surely avoid contact with you (and each other).

Silence prevails during the tour.

On a clear day, you'll see the city through the greenhouse windows that surround the Indoor Swamp. Little bridges and overpasses and tall buildings float by on all sides as the flat-bottomed boat makes its way down the river.

And, of course, you do go down at a steeper and steeper angle. The pace of the ride quickens. That's when you'll notice the Indoor Swamp getting narrower and... smaller. Fewer cypresses appear this far down the artificial river, and they are reduced. The all-encompassing Indoor Swamp seems to shrink before you by degrees. It finally resolves into what appears to be a model train set-sized landscape—the Indoor Swamp in miniature. At first, this optical illusion may make you sick to your stomach as you feel yourself descending even as you appear to be gliding upwards. This effect is exacerbated by the bits and pieces of the flat-bottomed boat shifting in and out of place under and around you. Its structure folds and rearranges itself like an origami figure. What was once a flat-bottomed boat soon resembles a series of narrow, connected roller coaster cars. No more need to avoid the other passengers. You will all be in single file, one car per person, as the tour continues.

The greenhouse and the cityscape beyond it rise until they disappear behind you into a large, dingy gray warehouse. The quality of the light changes from an outdoor glow to a drab, harsh fluorescent.

You never can tell exactly when the Indoor Swamp gives out and the flea market appears. The walls are dim. Little alcoves appear, filled with odd knickknacks, old books, and used furniture. The artificial mildew stench of the swamp gives way to the smell of bug spray.

All the items are used underneath the Indoor Swamp. Everything is for sale at a special price. But rarely will you discover anything of use. A child-size, crummy suitcase with crumbling innards. Ill-formed, glass globes filled with deformed black birds within ugly blue spirals. A crude ventriloquist dummy, hollow head half broken open—one good eye staring at you. Tacky, garish porcelain figures. Open, water damaged books too yellowed to read.

Of course, no one buys anything in the flea market. There are no clerks in the sale-nooks. But many of the sales materials are within easy reach, daring you to touch them. Now that you are no longer in danger of coming into contact with the other passengers, it's more tempting than ever. But you do so at your own risk.

The marketplace narrows, and the warehouse in which it's housed starts to fold in. You'll eventually find yourself in something like a trailer home in its atmosphere and width. What follows is the final and least pleasant aspect of the Indoor Swamp tour. But arguably the most thrilling. The flea market nooks disappear, replaced by rather drab looking rooms but for one or two disturbing objects within them.

Perhaps there is a room that contains a worn, vintage tea party set with frilly dressed dolls, but one of those doll's heads gradually rotates completely around, going from an expression of knowing, smiling perversion to an open-mouthed, silent O of horror and back again. Its eyes follow you as the doll's head slowly spins. Or the next room, a bedroom, might contain a large, black, corroded barrel in the place of a bed. A barrel that you are certain contains something so poisonous that you can feel and smell waves of sharp, nauseating dread peeling off of it. You may not be able to keep your eyes off such a barrel, not even to blink. Whatever is within might burst out, you think, like a Jack-in-the-Box the instant your attention shifts away.

The track propelling you forward through the tour slows to a crawl here. Long periods of low-ceilinged, claustrophobic tedium between rooms, punctuated by moments of panic. And then a final, dark room ahead. A room containing a kind of roaring abyss. After which you'll find yourself filing out with the crowd into a multi-level parking garage. The large, glass doors go dark and lock automatically as you and your fellow tour-goers exit.

You might find yourself frustrated, confused and deflated. You wouldn't be the first to dislike or even despise the Indoor Swamp. It's not for everyone. But you won't be able to resist a return trip.

On later visits to the Indoor Swamp you might find yourself staring through the greenhouse windows with longing. Those buildings and those slivers of sky around you look so bright. The busy, outside world seems so engaging. What a relief it would be, you might think, to be anywhere else beyond these glass walls. But you're filing back onto the long, flat boat. Making your way down the artificial lagoon. Skimming through the crummy flea market. Creeping along the trailer-hallway, viewing one disturbing mise en scène after another on your heavy way to that final abyss.

On subsequent visits, you might start voicing your complaints aloud to any of your companions who will listen. You're within your rights to do so as long as you don't break the "NO TOUCHING" rule.

"What are we doing here?" you might ask.

Don't be surprised when you receive no response from your fellow tour-goers. They'll be wrapped up in the moment or in daydreams about the thrilling bit before or the chilling bit ahead.

You may eventually begin to talk to yourself. And you may even have a hard time remembering certain things. How exactly did you arrive at the Indoor Swamp in the first place? And where do you go once you file into the multi-level parking garage at the end of the Indoor Swamp tour? You may find yourself after hours wandering through that half-lit labyrinth. So many other forlorn figures are slumping or staggering there, up and down dim stairwells and along empty parking spaces. It's a struggle to recall which vehicle you arrived in, let alone where you parked it. You may decide to simply wait in front of the large, glass entrance to the Indoor Swamp until the lights switch back on and the automatic lock disengages.

Sooner or later, you'll accept that the Indoor Swamp is the only show worth experiencing, or at least the only one you can access. Then you'll no longer gaze with longing at the buildings and slivers of sky beyond the Indoor Swamp's greenhouse windows. You might as well be in a real swamp in the acrid fog or in thin sunshine that never warms. Sooner or later, you'll be wrapped up in the moment or in daydreams about the thrilling bit before or the chilling bit ahead. It's the Indoor Swamp itself that has your full attention now. The descent as the Indoor Swamp flora shrinks into the dingy flea market below. The never available knickknacks within the Indoor Swamp flea market. The terrifying tableaus inside the innermost trailer-depths of the Indoor Swamp.

One day leads into the next in the Indoor Swamp. One familiar scene folds into another familiar scene in the Indoor Swamp.

The Indoor Swamp. It's a ride you can't miss... no matter how terribly you wish you could.

Origami Dreams

"I was cleaning a room and, meandering about, approached the divan and couldn't remember whether or not I had dusted it. Since these movements are habitual and unconscious, I could not remember and felt that it was impossible to remember… if the whole complex lives of many people go on unconsciously, then such lives are as if they had never been."

-Leo Tolstoy

"Everything that makes the world like it is now will be gone. We'll have new rules and new ways of living. Maybe there'll be a law not to live in houses, so then no one can hide from anyone else…"

-Shirley Jackson

N—,

I've made an odd discovery in the midst of my annual tidiness cleaning. You may remember those with some fondness, I hope. I was dusting the old hardwood underneath my bed when I noticed duct tape hanging from the box-spring. I peeled the rest of the semi-sticky material down, revealing a hole perhaps the size of a dime. My curiosity piqued, I stuck an index finger inside and came into contact with a folded, small cluster of papers, torn at the edges. I ended up needing to tear a much larger hole in the box-spring and pulled the paper figurine out, lined sheets that were crafted into a small house, origami-style.

I am disquieted, being the only owner of the box-spring in question and having lived alone for years before (with the sole exception of our all too brief years together). Moreover, the pages within don't appear to my expert eyes to be more than several years old, and, as you know, I've lived in this ranch-style house for thirty years and more.

When unfolded, I found the papers contained words, mostly filled out in a miniature, spidery longhand, that resemble neither your elegant script nor my careful cursive. These pages seem to be in the form of journal entries, though I question their nonfictional authenticity for reasons that will become obvious. I wonder if you'll have any insight on who wrote them or how they came to be squirreled away under the mattress that I've slept upon for so many years. The following is a transcription of the text.

This dream was special, *the journal began*, and I want to remember the details as I can recall them.

The days before our trip I had put in more hours at work than usual. I was supervising the movement of law library materials from the old firm to the new one. Trying to get everything done before the vacation, which of course just made things worse. I left an hour early, though, much to the relief of my coworkers. Margaret was standing at the picture window when I pulled up to the house, and soon we were on the Interstate and through the Foyle tunnel, towards the beach.

As Foyle receded, frowning behind us over the bay bridge, our mood became more relaxed. Margaret smiled, I think for the first time in weeks.

We just dropped the girls off to spend a week with their grandparents.

"I love em," Margaret said with a sigh. "but thank Christ they're gone." When she smiles, her eyes always crinkle—brown and almond shaped, the speckled, dark scar under one a reminder of Flight 389, the tragedy that plunged our lives into chaos over a decade ago. Margaret's neighborhood engulfed in fire and black smoke. I remember.

Nodding, I took her hand, and for once she didn't withdraw it. Within fifteen minutes—a sunset-sky clearing above the brisk but manageably trafficked superhighway—a hint of actual tranquility started to kick in.

Now, more than ever, we needed this break. The past year was a bad one. The tenth anniversary of the plane disaster. My big move from one law firm to another. The twins' constant whining and demands. I had lost myself in work. Sex fell off to nothing, and the fights had escalated.

Yeah, Margaret and I needed this break. Never mind that I always felt let down by the time we returned, waterlogged and vaguely depressed. I've often thought that the ideal vacation would be one in which nothing at all notable happened. Too often, though, "breaks" of this kind—those borrowed realities—are haunted by the *idea* of relaxation rather than the real thing. I was hoping this time things would be different. In the past, I've always hoped that.

The Interstate rumbled beneath us. Twilight. Margaret had fallen asleep next to me, and before I could think of pulling over I found my head also nodding off.

Next thing I knew our car was jerking upwards with an awful scraping sound as I awoke to find I had dozed and crossed the median.

Margaret screamed. I'm sure I did too.

An eighteen-wheeler, a blur of cars, SUVs and trucks whirred past us, horns dopplering to the left and right. A feeling of weightlessness. Time seemed to slow as I wrenched the car back and forth. And then everything... changed. The vehicles that had been careening around us were now traveling in the same direction as our car. It was as if the previous chaos had only been a kind of intricate illusion that cleared in the blink of an eye.

Margaret was no longer digging her nails into my arm, screaming, but now sat calm, silent and staring in the seat next to me. The Interstate, too, looked different. It was smaller and less trafficked, with only two instead of six lanes of traffic. More like a country highway.

At the time none of this seemed strange. I just remember looking for a turn I needed to make. I was in the left lane as a green exit sign popped up—hidden in the deep brush to my right. I made the sharp turn and realized almost too late that a beat up pickup truck was barreling the wrong way up the exit ramp towards us. I swerved onto the shoulder to avoid it, our car shuddering to a stop. The truck also screeched to a halt on the shoulder across from us. A wide-eyed, shock-haired young man got out of his pickup and ran towards our car. I started to drive on, thinking at first that he was drunk or enraged, but it became obvious the kid was upset for a different reason.

I rolled down the window and asked him if he was okay.

"Our house," the boy—no more than sixteen—said, adolescent voice cracking. In spite of his young age, his shaggy hair was solid white. "He's in our house."

"Who?"

"Daddy Longlegs," he replied, eyes wide.

"Your house is infested, son? You've got spiders?"

"No, sir—not spiders. Daddy Longlegs. A kind of ghost. Mama says only someone with six fingers on one hand can drive Daddy

Longlegs out."

Funny as it sounds, that's the first moment I considered I might be dreaming. For as long as I can remember, I've had an active dream life. And recently I've started training myself to become lucid during them.

Instead of responding to the kid, I immediately counted the fingers of my right hand and turned my head away for a moment. Then I counted them again, an exercise I had made a habit of repeating several times during the day and night. The idea: if you're dreaming, you'll count either more or less fingers than your hand has when you're awake. In this case, I counted six fingers.

There's a peculiar flush of pleasure that comes when you realize you're dreaming, that a kind of temporary reality is yours to control. This time, not only had I become aware of the dream—the dream itself had reminded me to count my fingers through the shock-haired boy. This was a peculiar one. A special one.

I considered changing the dream's narrative by force of will in that moment, but I was curious to see where my untethered imagination would take me. Besides, a life of dreaming had taught me that if I resisted the dream-flow, I might awaken prematurely. I knew I was more than likely asleep in my own bed with Margaret by my side, perhaps the night before our "real" vacation took place. Anyway, I thought. A lucid dream can be a vacation of a sort itself—a kind of borrowed reality—if mindfully experienced.

"It just so happens," I said, "that I excel in the exorcising of ghosts, demons and the like. What town is this?"

"Court Hill. Just follow me, sir. Poor mama's about to wriggle out of her skin."

"A wise man once observed, 'You're never upset for the reason you think.'"

As I followed the boy's battered truck down the wooded, country highway, large chunks from my dream life started coming to mind. I recalled one of the dream characters I often "played" was a dapper, older librarian. He specialized in learning secrets, usually of an occult nature. A name came to me: Solomon Kroth, Esoterician. I smiled with private amusement.

As we took a right turn into a downtown area, I began to feel certain that I had visited this picturesque resort town before. The architecture was in a preserved art deco style. Cobbled, Spanish moss covered, oak lined streets, well-manicured squares. I somehow knew that beyond the quaint City Hall lay a midsize lake, lined on three sides by dense forest. There were combination street light/clocks atop signs that proclaimed "Court Hill" in fancy script.

The next turn we made revealed gullies full of delicate ivy and crystalline hills topped by houses of unusual size and structure. It occurred to me that such geography was impossible in the flat, swampy mire I knew actually surrounded the east bank across from Foyle. Had I been awake, I thought, Court Hill would probably resemble one of those semi-rural towns—the kind that contain only a small grocery store and maybe a couple of combination convenience store/gas station/fast food establishments... the kind that dot the highways of the deep south.

The boy's truck finally turned into a long driveway between natural hedges, both sides of which almost met above us. As we drove down it—an unusually long way I thought—I counted the fingers of my right hand again, and the number of fingers once more added up to six. I remember thinking that was odd. There had also been an unusual, real-time consistency to the events so far, without the sudden leaps from one scene to the next so typical in dreams. The lighting that surrounded us, though, had remained in a static, twilit state ever since we had pulled off onto the shoulder of the exit ramp. Darkness had never fallen. That at least was reassuring.

At last, the haunted structure came into view within a large clearing. It was a slim, tall cottage with a prominent front door set between two narrow windows. The house couldn't have been more than fifteen feet wide and jutted up from the ground like a spearhead. Ivy or kudzu grew over three quarters of the very high peaked gable.

I remembered Margaret for the first time since we pulled off of the Interstate and turned to ask her what she thought of the place. But she was staring at the house in front of us, mouth open, terrified. Without thinking, I placed my six-fingered hand on her stomach and muttered some arcane phrase under my breath. Suddenly, I could see through her eyes, as if gazing through binoculars. The cottage before us was unfolding like deconstructed origami paper. Within seconds a stick figure loomed over our car where the house had stood, a figure so thin it hurt. A razor sharpness in those limbs.

I did something to Margaret's arm then—squeezing a pressure point, I think. Whatever it was, she fell asleep, her form becoming flat and diminished. I opened the car door. The cottage had resumed its original form through my own eyes, but I could feel the giant, sharp, stick figure in every excruciating angle of it.

In spite of the supernatural turn of events, I smiled, knowing I was only inhabiting a borrowed reality, a new but temporary story and stock set piece. And now, I thought, it was time to take control.

"Houses dream, did you know that?" I asked the shock-haired boy who followed me, head bowed (perhaps in prayer). "All things dream, to one degree or another. And sometimes our waking selves share dreams of the darkened hollow, the deep forest, city squares. Like them, houses dream, and when those dreams are nightmares, we call them haunted. This is such a house."

"But what does that have to do with Daddy Longlegs?" The boy asked. "He comes through the corners. Makes you hear and see things that hurt."

"Those sights and sounds are manifestations of this house's dreams, son, and houses dream so slowly. Those dreams could last for decades or until the house falls apart or burns down leaving a cold heap of ashes that animals and children shun."

We entered the house, which consisted of one large and very high single room. It was meticulously neat in there, painted white. Bright halogen lights hung from the cathedral-style ceiling.

"So do we burn it down?" the boy asked. "Mama ain't gonna like that."

"No indeed. We must *wake it up.*"

As we approached the center of the house, I heard a rustling from the walls and ceiling, as if from an epic rodent infestation.

"Do you hear that, my boy?" I asked. "That is the house talking in its sleep."

A kind of sterility was at odds with the eerie presence of Daddy Longlegs (or the Origami, as I had internally dubbed it). I avoided certain corners that looked sharp-edged or untidy. I closed my eyes, listening to the continuous rustling around me. And I understood it.

"I know its name now. Son, you'll want to leave and collect your family. By the time you get back, I'll be gone, and your problem will be solved."

The boy nodded and left. And when I turned back from the front door, I felt the house unfolding around me. The spectral figure of the Origami loomed. I (as Solomon Kroth, Esoterician) was undaunted.

"This dream is over."

I expected to wake up in my bed then, basking in the glow of a fascinating and satisfying dream fantasy. Prepared at last for a successful, real world vacation. But I didn't awaken.

I now could see myself in third person—Kroth, an imposing and dapper, bow-tied, older gentlemen with a shaggy, well-trimmed quaff of grey hair. My mouth opened and spoke the house's secret name. And I felt a great cracking noise.

When I came to myself again, the Origami figure had disappeared, and the house's structure was changing before my eyes. The sterile brightness of the room was fading, the hanging halogens winking out like stars at dawn. In their place, dingy lamps appeared, white walls bleeding into thin particleboard. The flawless looking brick floors morphed into an unpleasant gray shag carpet. The vaulted ceiling sagged into a low, wrinkled one.

While the house was still righting itself, still awakening by degrees, I stepped outside. Night had fallen at last, and the cicadas were shrieking all around me in large cypress trees, blanketed with Spanish moss. The air was heavy with moisture. I felt no need to look back at the house as I approached our car, which was parked outside on a red dirt road. My wife was undiminished and fast asleep within.

I settled into our car and counted my fingers again. Five on each hand no matter how many times I looked away and recounted them all. My assumption had been that I was still dreaming. But now I had the heady, chilling (but not altogether unpleasant) realization that I may not have been dreaming at any point. Which begged the questions—where were we now? And where had we been?

After some minor trouble and travel through a nondescript town called Daphne, I found the Interstate again. I headed back towards the beach, my head oddly tranquil as Margaret awoke, smiled and took my (now unaltered) hand.

"You've been out for a while, baby," I said. "Hey, did you have any weird dreams while you were out?"

Margaret looked at me quizzically. "Not that I can remember. Was I talking in my sleep?"

"Well, yeah. You seemed kind of scared at one point, y'know?"

"Huh."

"Feeling okay now, babe?"

"Actually, yeah. Feel like I've already had a good night's sleep. We close?"

"Yep. And I think this vacation is gonna be great."

"Know what, hon?" she asked, giving my hand a squeeze, her almond eyes flashing in the headlights of an approaching car. "I do too."

And it has been great. In fact, it's been the best vacation we've ever had.

I'm writing this now on the balcony overlooking the Gulf waves in the cool morning light. I feel calm and well rested. It's tranquility at odds, I know, with the uncanny events at "Court Hill." Speaking of which, Margaret has no recollection of our near accident on the Interstate, let alone anything about the Origami house. I wonder what our return home will bring. Things feel so different now between Margaret and me here at the beach. I can't recall us ever getting along so well.

I've kept my cell off the whole time. Haven't even been tempted to check my messages or go online, even to check on the kids. I can't help wishing we could stay here permanently, as unrealistic as that sounds.

Confession: I don't miss the girls at all, and I think Margaret feels the same way. That's terrible. I know. I should really erase that thought.

Postscript.

Some days later. Something's wrong with Margaret. I think she may be falling apart all over again, just like she did post-Flight 389.

The trip home itself was uneventful until we passed over the bay bridge. I could feel Margaret shifting uneasily next to me.

"That's weird," she said.

"What's weird?"

"That big greenhouse thing."

We were passing through Foyle's central business district. Sure enough, the handful of mid-size skyscrapers and hotels seemed to be surrounding a glassed-in edifice I hadn't noticed before.

"Huh," I replied. "Must be something new connected to the aquarium."

"I thought I saw people on a boat going down a river in there."

"You okay, babe?" The double, vertical lines of anxiety had appeared between Margaret's dark brows. Hadn't seen those since the morning we left for the beach.

"Yeah, just... things look kinda different. I dunno, like we've been gone for years instead of days."

"Well, a wise man once said, 'home looks different in the afterglow of a successful vacation.'"

Margaret scowled, the scar under her eye pinching. "Who said that? I've never heard that."

And then the cold hard distance was back between us again, as if our dream vacation never had been.

We picked up the girls, both of whom were louder and more temperamental than ever. Within minutes, Margaret was screaming at them to shut up. The girls sulked and pouted for a few minutes before the whining and bickering amped back up. And Margaret screamed at them again.

The rest of the way home, between the family drama scenes, I noticed how odd Margaret was behaving, staring at the grocery stores, gas stations, shops, and parks with growing alarm.

"That wasn't an abandoned lot. A park there?" I heard her murmuring to herself.

Things got worse once we reached our neighborhood and our house.

"Where are you going? This isn't our street. That isn't our home," Margaret said, almost hysterical. One of the girls started to cry.

"Baby, just... just hold it together. We'll be inside soon."

"But where are we? Where the fuck are we, Jack?"

Our two-story home sat among the others in a semi-rural neighborhood, just as it always had.

"What's wrong, mommy?" One of the twins asked.

"Nothing's wrong sweetheart. Mommy's just tired." I reached over to pat Margaret's hand, and she tore it away.

"Don't touch me and don't try to make this alright, Jack. There's something wrong here. Something wrong with everything."

It was dark, but the house did look slightly different to me as we pulled up to it. It could've been my imagination, but the two-story, sprawling edifice seemed elongated and shorter.

"Look, we're all tired and stressed, sweetie. Let's just get the kids inside, eat a bite and go to bed."

"Stop fucking telling me what to do, Jack," she said, exiting the car and storming towards the back door, fumbling with her keys.

Margaret is now in the guest bedroom. I can hear her talking to herself. I'm going to call the psychiatrist tomorrow morning. This behavior isn't entirely unprecedented, but I haven't seen her this bad in a decade—maybe not even then. She's delusional. There's nothing different about our house.

As I sit here in my study, though, I've got to admit that a couple of things do seem off here. The picture window next to the living room looks onto unfamiliar, untidy shapes in the darkness. I can't place them. And some of the corners near the fireplace look askew somehow.

It occurs to me that maybe I'm dreaming. I keep counting my fingers and only come up with five on each hand no matter how many times I look away and count again. I'm sure it's just nerves and disappointment. Worse than usual post-vacation depression. Maybe things will look up tomorrow.

———

A good while has passed since my last entry. I'm not sure how long.

The morning after my last entry, Margaret was still agitated but no longer talking, her eyes wide, staring at everything (even me and the kids) askance. At breakfast, when pressed, she would only ask me a series of questions.

"Did you notice how many smokestacks there are in town? When did Municipal Park become that large? Do you remember so many ranch style houses on Cypress Street?"

I didn't answer, lost in thought, busily trying to get the girls ready for school. The girls. They looked different post-vacation somehow—older, one skinnier than I remembered. Both strange in mood and personality.

I had trouble getting them off to the bus. Had completely forgotten the routine. TV, breakfast, clothes, tooth brushing, what else? In no time I was late for work. Margaret offered no help at all, staring at the breakfast table, uneaten oatmeal in front of her, muttering.

I left soon after, directing the girls to wait for the school bus. I didn't conduct my typical goodbye ritual, distracted by the odd landscape outside.

Margaret was right after all. The neighborhood, the streets, everything around our home appeared altered. An aging playground where a corner shoe store had been. An empty parking lot backing up to what might be a warehouse of some sort. Unfamiliar. I had quite a time just navigating the streets, many of which had peculiar names.

Instead of going straight on to work, I decided to drive to the University Library near my law firm. Once there, I haunted the reference department—scanning through the shelves of the Special Collections behind the circulation desk, rolling through miles of microfilm. All in an attempt to find any hint of what was happening to our city. I wasn't surprised that Court Hill on the eastern shore had never existed—only the small, rural hamlet of Daphne. Nor did I ever find any reference to a Daddy Longlegs ghost or Origami house or any interesting or applicable cases that related to my weird experience. But I was certain the changes in everything were related to it somehow.

Time passed. Again, I'm not sure how much because I began experiencing sudden jumps from one day to another. I know I didn't go back to the law firm that week, and I don't remember getting any calls or messages of concern from my peers. I didn't bother contacting them either. Each day I simply returned to the university library, spending my time online in the small study offices within the reference department.

Life, such as it was, became a blur. Late nights returning home found Margaret locked in the guest bedroom or standing in front of the living room's picture window, unmoving and staring at the alien world outside. The mornings, too, bled into one another. Redundant stress patterns. The children becoming even stranger to me.

And then one morning the girls weren't in their bedroom at all. Or anywhere in or around the house.

I went into a panic, of course, and pleaded with (and eventually railed against) the local police force—the Second District. I think they've blocked my number, but I've continued sending them stern letters with unheeded warnings. But the school doesn't have a record of either of the girls anymore. One evening I came home from the library and found I couldn't even remember their names. I still can't. Nor have I been able to find any documents, birth certificates or otherwise, to prove they ever existed. Their bedroom is now a storeroom. All that remains of them are broken images and a hollow grief. Margaret offered no help.

"It doesn't matter," she said one night, her voice no more than a whisper, the scar under her dark eyes shining in the moonlight. "They weren't my girls. Not at all. And you... you're not my Jack. Not anymore."

Margaret was standing in our living room day and night by then, blankly staring out of the picture window. And when she wasn't at the window, she was asleep on the living room couch—flat and diminished. I tried to get her help, tried calling shrinks in town dozens of times, but a peculiar forgetfulness always got in my way. I would set up an appointment for her in the morning and then fail to remember all the details of it after a hard day at the library. Late that night or even a week later, I would realize with a start that I still needed to get help for Margaret. Between those moments of lucidity, though, my head spun with esoteric details about Foyle and the surrounding area. What had happened to the children, to me, to Margaret, to our lives? I was possessed with a driving need to find out.

I discovered how much Foyle itself was changing—an encroaching industrial area once well to the north of town merging into an ever growing city park. The air quality had worsened, leading to days of thick, toxic fog growing in length and severity. My health—never a problem before—began declining, leading to frequent coughing fits. I even managed to secure some old oxygen tanks from somewhere (I can't recall). But my research continued unabated, paradoxically the only respite I had from my home-based grief and horror.

The gaps or jumps in time increased in frequency and severity. Hours or even days passed without my being conscious of where I had been or what I had been doing.

It was following one of those time gaps that I realized Margaret, like our girls before her, had disappeared from the house. I fell immediately into a profound depression that led to the brink of suicide. While I was lucid one morning, I made myself insulate every untidy crack or crevice in the house. Bath towels and plastic bags lined the bottoms of the front and back doors. I headed to the kitchen with the intent to open the oven and extinguish its pilot light, and then, with a start, I found myself back in the library. A new, frenetic energy had possessed me in the interval, and I was back on the search. I ordered and consumed interlibrary loan books on lucid dreaming, ventriloquism and environmental disasters in between doing research on a local, abandoned paper mill that I felt sure was connected somehow.

Once, I became aware of my surroundings while on my way to the library. I was backing out of the driveway and spotted the figure of Margaret staring vacantly out of our living room window. But when I dashed into the house, no one was there.

And then one day I woke up to find a strange woman sleeping next to me in my own bed, who claimed to have lived with me as a partner for years. She said her name was N— and called me Sol. I responded with angry denials and threats. After the woman finally left in confused, astonished tears, I spent the rest of the day screaming and sobbing and gasping on the couch of the living room, as if I had lost Margaret and the girls all over again.

Not long ago, I forced myself to drive out to my law firm, which I hadn't seen since our last vacation. Instead, I found myself parking as usual behind the university library. My law firms—both old and new—were simply gone. When I looked up the agency addresses in the reference department, I saw that both had been replaced by a shabby dentist's office and a second-hand clothing store respectively. The partners, associates and paralegals I worked with were no more. Now aging, shabby librarians and a handful of vacant undergraduate assistants were my coworkers. Everyone called me

Mr. Kroth, and my reflection confirmed the man I had become: an imposing but dapper, bow-tied, older gentlemen all in tweed with a well-trimmed quaff of increasingly white hair. I counted my fingers. Five fingers on each hand. But in lucid moments at home I have heard a rustling and something strange about the corners of the sitting room—an untidiness. A filth smoldering or unfolding within and around the fireplace. But only in my peripheral vision.

This hideous, one-story ranch-style house no longer resembles the expansive two-story Margaret, the girls and I once lived in. I would move if I could concentrate or moderate my compulsive need to research the strange phenomena going on in and around Foyle. But my mental lapses are starting to increase in frequency and length. I might be laboring at the library when the idea of taking a trip out of town—perhaps to the beach—occurs to me. And suddenly I'll awaken in the middle of the night, sweating, to discover the next morning that another week has passed. At times I seem only a part time spectator of my own life, as in the kind of dreams that shift from first to third person and back. Watching the sad, lonely old Esoterician going through his rounds as his jumbled life and health falls apart. At these times I am not in control of my own actions, and Kroth appears to be subject to a kind of unwanted mania—writing and talking to skeptical, local officials about the arcane, environmental transformations and conspiracies and crimes that seem to be taking place all over this despicable city.

Some days I feel more lucid than others, though, and at these times the bottom drops out of my mood. I call in sick from work at the library and spend the day puttering about the house, trying to remember what it looked like before Court Hill and the Origami changed the foundation of its existence. On these days I imagine killing myself in the most vivid ways every time I close my eyes. On these days I spend an inordinate amount of time staring at all the unclean corners of this alien house. I know it's changing by degrees—unfolding perhaps. In no time at all, it seems, a nervous mania or mental lapse assails me, and I'm swept days or weeks away again out of my body and mind. I've become a helpless spectator of an unfamiliar reality, unable to take any but the most trivial action.

I am aware that the insane often insist on their sanity, and I am doubly aware that these experiences of mine seem like mad ones. If these are indeed delusions, they are of a kind and consistency about which I'm unfamiliar. As when I tried to seek psychological help for Margaret, I can't seem to concentrate on arranging permanent or even palliative mental healthcare for myself. I'll dial the number of such a provider and forget why I called or start to engage the hapless individual on the other side of the line in nonsense about factories, mutated skeletons, corrupt police-cultists, even ventriloquist dummies. Only after I hang up do I remember that I need help, desperately, and then the sorry routine repeats itself.

Just yesterday, I woke up to find a vestigial nub of a sixth finger on my right hand. The sight of it enraged me, and I started trashing the inside of this mocking house—all its awful Hummel figurines and cheap, floral themed paintings—and for a time I felt like me again. I even willed myself into Kroth's old, sensible Volvo and hit the Interstate for the beach. But as I crossed the Foyle Bay Bridge, my resolve began to waver. I could sense the Kroth-self struggling to get back to its important work. I could sense my foot struggling to hit the brakes, and my hands trembling with a desire to take the next exit so I could turn back towards Foyle and its university library. Instead, through sheer force of will, I slammed my foot on the gas and swerved across the median. I don't know if the impulse was suicidal or borne out of sick curiosity or was simply beyond my control altogether.

I veered to avoid oncoming traffic in spite of my fervent wish to die at that moment. Just as so long ago (it seemed), vehicles blurred around me, their horns dopplering left and right. Weightlessness. I clenched my eyes closed in a last attempt at oblivion. But when I opened them again, I was traveling down a familiar country highway. All the traffic moving in my direction. In spite of the fact that I knew it was still mid-morning, everything was suffused in an orange-pink twilight. As I had before, I veered to the right and found myself on the Court Hill exit, but there appeared no shock-haired boy driven truck barreling towards me. Instead, I continued down the exit and found a rough, gravel street and, from a strangely vivid memory, made a sharp right. Court Hill itself looked unrecognizable. No quaint downtown area of any kind—no cobbled streets or well-manicured squares. No quaint city hall building, peculiar streetlight-signs or any sign of a lake. But I did see hills and gullies covered in thick waves of kudzu—the impossible hills surmounted with slender, tall houses, which stared at me with a dreadful, collective presence. They had awakened. And in spite of a spectral, twilit beauty, an intrinsic bleakness infused everything, as if even the green life surrounding me had become an expression of its opposite. Some of the houses—which appeared to be replicas of each other—I noticed had residents inside them. Like my poor Margaret, they stood empty eyed on the other side of tall, thin windows.

I tried to turn around, tried to force myself to stop the car. But all control had been subliminally relinquished, and I had become a mere dream-spectator in a reality that was not a dream. I made the final, automatic turn towards what I felt was the center of town—the source of the foul awakening. But the Origami house appeared now to be nothing more than a trailer, battered and falling apart, almost at one with the kudzu that smothered it. And then the trailer unfolded itself. And unfolded itself. And unfolded itself.

I'm no longer certain of what happened next. A voice (my voice?) spoke to me in whispers and rustlings and screams.

I wasn't surprised that I came to myself—such as I am—later, traveling back over the bay bridge. I could smell the city before I could see it, passing a sign that proclaimed, "Welcome to Dunnstown! Next to Yours, the Best Town in the United States!" Foyle as I knew it was gone. I drove towards a smoggy little city with factories and expansive parks and one indoor swamp nestled within its central business district. The voice of the Origami, the thing that the shock-haired boy had called Daddy Longlegs, echoes still within my mind, a static that imparts so much more than words ever could. In certain moods, I feel a vast sense of relief. It's all out of my hands now. Has never truly been in my hands. But at other times I'm wracked with guilt. I somehow awakened one sleeping house in Court Hill. And now everything on both the east and west shores is waking up into a new, malignant reality. There is no possibility of flight, to the beach or elsewhere. I belong to Dunnstown.

I continue my work in the library, and I am still subject to awful bouts of nervous mania punctuated by suicidal depression. But more and more I become lost in the thought of Dunnstown itself, the terrible plane catastrophe most Dunnstowners can only half remember, the police conspiracy to cover up a new and terrible series of occult-based crimes. An abandoned factory in the midst of the city's park that contains a miserable secret. I've become lost in what passes for Solomon Kroth's esoteric life. I am awakening by degrees into this not-dream in which mortuaries and chapels are full and not even the air itself may be breathed freely.

As I sit at my desk in the reference department, puffing occasionally on one of my oxygen tanks, I count the fingers of my right hand out of force of habit. The vestigial finger on my right hand disappeared or fell off some time ago. The once familiar memories of Foyle, what was my house, Margaret, the twins, everything I thought I was and knew are fading. I'm going to burn this journal or at least hide it out sight so that the memories might fade more quickly. In my more lucid moments I know that this life, such as it is, will not last much longer. The man I once was would consider that a mercy, but I no longer even believe in the release of death. It is only a transition into yet another borrowed reality.

So that's what I found within a series of folded papers inside my bed, N—. I've never before been able to explain why I forced you out of the house in the midst of our serene, loving life, and I don't expect belief, understanding or forgiveness to come of this letter. I just want to know that you're still out there, that things aren't changing again. Here in Dunnstown every autumn that comes around brings longer and fouler paper mill days. Do you remember those, or are they too only new ripples of chaos in the fabric of things? More hidden or forgotten realities waking up out of the dream of today.

Please write me back, N—. My health is failing, I've developed a terrible stutter, and I've been blacking out for days at a time. Even if you only return the enclosed self-addressed stamped envelope to let me know you're alive. That you ever existed. I feel everything slipping away into a new world—a blacker reality than any I've ever known or felt. Half the days I don't know who I am anymore, and I'm afraid that the powers that be in Dunnstown—or the powers behind the powers that be—are changing things again. Daddy Longlegs, the Origami... folding and unfolding inside. Help me, N—
.

As I look over this spidery script, I can feel my perspective slipping from first person to third, and I'm wondering if this old, shock-haired librarian isn't me at all. Perhaps Solomon Kroth—that silly, lonely Esoterician—is only a part of what I am. Perhaps I exist within the texture of these walls, the low, sagging ceilings of these pages. I can feel the structure shift as it all changes again.

I would count my fingers to see if I'm still dreaming. But I have so many.

20 Simple Steps to Ventriloquism

Being a ventriloquist is a lot of fun. Anyone from eight to eighty can learn the basic techniques of this craft with a little practice. If you really want to know about ventriloquism and what it can do for you, just follow these 20 easy steps, and one day you will find out just how much fun a ventriloquist can have.

STEP 1
"How to hold your mouth"

Always practice in front of a mirror. Close your mouth in a natural, relaxed way and part your lips slightly. Stare at your mouth in this position until you can see nothing else, as if your mouth were hovering in the midst of nothingness.

STEP 2
"Recite the beginner's alphabet"

The first part of the beginner's alphabet has 19 letters. The letters are: A, C, D, E, G, H, I, J, K, L, N, O, Q, R, S, T, U, X, and Z. With your mouth in the position described in STEP 1, recite this part of the alphabet over and over. You may have to do this hundreds or even thousands of times before you get it right. While you master this STEP, it may seem strange that these sounds are coming out of your mouth while it is not moving. Try not to focus on this phenomenon or your progress as a ventriloquist may be hindered.

STEP 3
"Your first sentence"

The second part of the alphabet has 7 letters: B, F, M, P, V, W, and
Y. If you try to pronounce these letters the same way you did the
others, you will find that you have to move your lips. So, for the
time being, substitute another sound for these letters. For example,
try this sentence: "The bad boy destroyed the big jet by using his
brain." Only with your mouth in the position described in STEP 1,
say: "The **d**ad **d**oy destroyed the **d**ig jet **d**y using his **d**rain." Again,
focus strictly on your technique, avoiding any other thoughts or
perceptions you may have.

STEP 4
"You say one thing... and think another"

Think of the letter "B" while you are saying the letter "D." If you sit in front of the mirror long enough and say the letter "D" while thinking "B," you will soon have a sound clear enough so that, in normal conversation, no one will notice the difference. Even you may soon fail to notice that you are saying one thing and thinking another, as this technique becomes second nature to you.

STEP 5
"Use 'TH' or 'ETH' instead of 'F'"

Instead of saying "F" make it come out "eth" if it comes in the
middle or end of a word. If it comes at the beginning of a word, just
say "th." Example: "Without any effort, I frankly feel like a trifle."
Now say "Without any ethort, I thrankly theel like a trithle." This is
where the real challenge of ventriloquism begins as you practice over
and over—many thousands of times—in front of a mirror. For a
while you will sound as if you have a speech impediment and may
not even recognize your own voice. But do not give up. Later your
voice will become your "dummy voice," which will be nothing like
the voice you recognize as your own.

STEP 6
"How to say the letters 'M', 'P', and 'V'"

Instead of saying "M" say "N." Try this sentence: "My mind made the mad rummy melt." This is not difficult, for "N" is a combination of "M" and "N" as you say, "**N**y **n**ind **n**ade the **n**ad ru**nn**y **n**elt." Even though most of us have never made a "mad rummy melt" with our "mind," this is all part of the act of "dummy talk." Do the same with "P"—using "T" in its place. For the sentence, "The proud teacher put his pupil together," say "The troud teacher tut his tutil together." For "V" use "The"—while you think "V." For the sentence, "Not every ventriloquist is a Greater Ventriloquist," say "Not e**the**ry **the**ntriloquist is a Greater **The**ntriloquist." Of course, you may think this is all complete nonsense, but a lot of things that people say—even most things—are complete nonsense. This is not the ventriloquist's concern.

STEP 7
"'W' is tricky, but you can do it"

If you say the letter "W" as it sounds, it will come out as "dubble-you." That's fairly easy, isn't it? You know now to say "duddle-you" instead. But now take the word "wish," as in "I wish I was a Greater Ventriloquist," which you cannot say without a flutter of the lips, not even if you say it many thousands of times. So here is where you will need practice. Make a sound—something like "OHISH." Say it over and over until it sounds enough like "WISH" so that it can pass for this word, just as so many things pass for other things in this world.

STEP 8
"Getting to know your dummy"

Sit down on a chair in front of a mirror and carefully put your
ventriloquist dummy on your knee. Hold on to your dummy with
both hands. Insert your right or left hand into its back and find its
controls. Practice moving its head and its mouth. Think about your
dummy moving its head while *you* move its head. Think about its
mouth opening and closing while *you* open and close it. Soon you
will be performing these actions without having to put them
together in your head. That is how your dummy needs to move.
Automatically. Its eyes must move around, scanning the room just
like yours might. Its mouth must open and close in perfect concert
with your unconscious voice throwing (see STEPS 1-7). This STEP
may take more than hundreds or even thousands of *hours* to perfect
as you stare at yourself and your dummy in the mirror. After enough
practice, the dummy will move just as easily and as naturally as you
do.

STEP 9
"They are all dummies"

STEP 8 directed you to practice using your dummy until it moved "as naturally as you do." But how can a block of wood, carved and painted in the likeness of a human being, ever hope to be natural? Before we explore the answer to this crucial question, you are going to need to answer a question of a different but no less crucial sort. *What do you wish to achieve through the art of ventriloquism?* If your aim is simply to become a proficient showman, skilled enough to achieve some modicum of success through performing at children's birthday parties, local variety shows and community theatre acts, do not read any further. Study and apply STEPS 1-8 but *do not read on.* Your tutelage is complete, and with enough practice you very well may become a competent, even an excellent, show business ventriloquist. *However*, if STEPS 1-8 do not satisfy you, if manipulating your dummy seems limited and simplistic and even frustrating, if you have an overwhelming desire—a hunger—to know what Greater Ventriloquism is and what it can do for you and your life, read on. *Again: you must continue reading only if you really want to know what the secret of Greater Ventriloquism has to offer.* Fine. Now that *that* is out of the way—again: how *can* a block of wood, carved and painted in the likeness of a human being, ever hope to be natural? Easy. Have you ever had a pet? Many at-home animals are taught to behave using commands—which may be direct (like "stay" or "sit") but which might also involve subtle gestures and sounds, all of which you may make without conscious thought. You "push their levers" and "pull their cords" so to speak, to make them do what you want them to do. With practice, we can control our pets without effort, without thinking about it. We do one thing and think another. And what about our relationships with other *human* animals? Cannot we "push their levers" and "pull their cords" just as well, just as automatically?

Is this manipulation really all that different from making your ventriloquist dummy move and talk—just how you want it to move and saying just what you want it to say? If you practice STEPS 1-8 for very long, you will learn all you need to know about controlling the animals around you—human or not—bar none. STEP 9 is your first *real* step towards becoming a Greater Ventriloquist, but it is quite a simple one. Just remind yourself that the ventriloquist dummy, your pets, your family and friends all have one thing in common with each other: they are *dummies*. With practice, you will be amazed at how they will dance to the tune of your voice.

STEP 10
"Do not be discouraged"

As you work to control all the animal-dummies around you as
prescribed in STEP 9 ("They are all dummies"), it may soon appear
that they are not sentient at all. You may observe how artificial their
thoughts and motivations appear, from their impulses to eat and
sleep to the redundant static of their words. But you may also have
noticed how difficult it is to control animal-dummies for any length
of time. This is normal. The fact is, no matter how meticulous or
consistent your practice is, it is practically impossible to make an
animal-dummy move and speak just the way you want it to move
and speak. And it is painful and exhausting to try. But do not be
discouraged. Suffering and exhaustion are both key to your future
mastery of Greater Ventriloquism.

STEP 11
"Remove yourself from animal-dummies"

Have you practiced STEPS 1-10? Have you practiced these STEPS every day? Have you spent uncountable hours in front of the mirror throwing your voice, lips never fluttering? Does your dummy have a life and a voice as real to you as any animal-dummy—human or non-human—you have ever known? Can you do one thing while thinking about something else (or even nothing at all)? Have you at least *tried* to influence or control the so-called sentient beings around you? If not, do not bother reading on—you are not ready yet. However, if you *have* earnestly attempted to master STEPS 1-10 as described above, *it is imperative that you immediately remove yourself from daily contact with other animals—human or not.* Since you have made the choice to pursue Greater Ventriloquism, you have likely discovered that managing your ventriloquism practice and "real world" activities and relationships simultaneously is a difficult if not impossible task. Are the basic instructions stated in STEP 9 ("They are all dummies") erroneous then? Not at all. On the contrary, *trying* to master STEP 9 is essential to your growth towards becoming a Greater Ventriloquist. Even if you fail after tens of thousands of attempts (and—believe me—you will), this practice and this practice alone will lead you to STEP 12... and beyond.

STEP 12
"Find a good place to work"

STEP 12 goes hand in hand with STEP 11: find yourself a good, isolated place to live without comfort and communication contraptions—where you and your dummy can have all the time in the world unmolested. You may have to pull a few strings and put some things together to make this happen. The choices that must be made in the name of Greater Ventriloquism sometimes require sacrifices that come in all manner of forms. In fact, a potential Greater Ventriloquist at times must perform actions that the common herd of animal-dummies may find unsavory—even criminal—in nature. This is not your concern. Remember, the "people" you must deal with to survive are mere dummies serving a higher purpose—a kind of Ultimate Ventriloquism—that they cannot hope to comprehend. Animal-dummies must be treated at all times with false and/or unsympathetic regard. Believe me, they do not feel a thing.

STEP 13
"Mirror-work"

Your most dramatic transition from lesser to Greater Ventriloquism begins now. Choose or otherwise attain a mirror, one in a space that can be made to be almost completely devoid of natural light. Of course, you must have some form of light for your work, but it must be quite dim. Try a tiny lamp bulb wrapped in a dark blue gel of the sort used for dressing backstage. It will need to be put together. The illumination must be sparse enough so that you can only just barely see yourself and your dummy in the mirror the first time you turn out your primary light source. If possible, procure a tape player or some such contraption and record the next STEP as if it were a meditation or relaxation exercise (even if you know that attempting to achieve Greater Ventriloquism is anything but meditative or relaxing). Replay this recording in the semi-darkness of your mirror-space until you achieve the desired results. It may take many attempts, literally *thousands* of attempts, to accomplish the ultimate goal of this most exciting and challenging STEP yet, but with enough practice you will do just fine.

STEP 14
"The dummy is a trifle"

It is best not to think about what must come next. Simply listen to this voice guiding you on and let go. Without effort, completely let go. By now, you should be able to see a shadowy, slightly glowing reflection of yourself and your dummy in the mirror. Look at your dummy, sitting on your knee as always, in the mirror's reflection. Now set it carefully on a chair next to yours. Make sure it is stable. Make sure you can see the dummy's whole head reflected in the mirror. Set its eyes to look straight into your eyes. Now make sure for the remainder of the lesson that you are not touching it in any way. *The dummy is a trifle. It is nothing.* Stare at your dummy. Clear your mind of everything *but* your dummy on the stool in the mirror in front of you, specifically its eyes. Consider those eyes (*they are nothing*), but now think about the other side of them that you cannot see (the eye swivel mechanism attached to the cords that run down its head into the grooves in the control handle within your dummy's otherwise hollow body). *The dummy is a trifle. It is nothing.* Gently clear your mind of all thought. Stare at your dummy without blinking. As you consider your dummy's perfectly still form in the mirror, your eyes may burn; your pulse rate may increase—an unpleasant feeling that you are getting too little air—a squeezing sensation up and down your torso as if something is twisting inside you. You may begin to imagine you hear something like static or even the roar of an airliner. You may feel lightheaded, like you are going to pass out. Ignore these feelings. They are normal. They indicate that you are coming into perfect sync with the dummy's empty body and empty head (*it is a trifle*). Your own body and mind and all its living organs will resist communion with this dead matter. Clear your mind of that pain and panic and replace it with a perfect schematic of your dummy's eyes and the mechanism within them. Do not blink. Do not move. Now... when you have lost all sense of where you are or even *what* you are, conscious only of your dummy, *make your dummy's eyes move*. How? After all those hundreds of weeks and those thousands of hours, moving your dummy is no different than moving your legs. Your body is no longer limited to the bag of meat and bones you were born into. Now... *put yourself together*. The first time it happens you will not remember seeing those dummy eyes shifting to its left. You will see the dummy's eyes right up until you *know* they are about to move, and suddenly it seems that you are no longer looking at the dummy at all. You did it. You will find the undeniable reality: those dummy eyes have indeed moved from their original position. And not only did they move to the left, but—just for a moment—you seemed to be looking out of those glassy, dummy eyes yourself. Being sick to your stomach now is perfectly normal.

STEP 15
"No more dummies"

Ventriloquists talk to themselves and Greater Ventriloquists talk to themselves even when they are not actually talking. It is a fact—an inescapable side effect of all those thousands of practice sessions staring at yourself in a mirror; all those thousands of hours spent manufacturing a pretend-relationship with a doll or with their animal-dummy cohorts. But by now you should be stripped of these delusions of dummy-identity. You know *it and they are trifles*. And it is high time to dispense with these toys and sentimental trappings and get down to real work. No more dummies at all.

STEP 16
"See the world"

There were some surprises after you mastered STEP 14 ("The dummy is a trifle"). Surprise 1: ever since you mastered STEP 14, your stomach is a wreck, and you are not eating or drinking much. That is normal. Surprise 2: you have lost your ability to throw your voice or make your dummy move in any conventional sense. You have tried to *force* the dummy to speak a couple of times out of what you imagined was sheer boredom, but you discovered that the sound of the dummy's voice had terribly changed the several times you tried it—a horribly painful noise to the ear, like radio static layered across the tortured squeal of failing brakes on a car. I would say that is normal, but I am not sure that it is. What does it matter, though? Throwing your voice—pah—simple steps any fool could master. You have gone far beyond those parlor tricks now. Surprise 3: you know deep down just what the dummy is going to do before it does it. Don't you? *More static.* Try not to be anxious about all of this static. *It is a trifle.* Speaking of which—you know what that old dummy of yours would say if it was still talking? "Get out of here, animal-dummy," it would say. "See the world and show 'em what ya got." The dummy is right, isn't it? Thanks to your tremendous powers of Greater Ventriloquism, you can do almost anything.

STEP 17
"Controlling animal-dummies... and beyond"

Start with that street bum—the one you may have seen many times before lurking on these seedy streets. Just relax and take one step at a time. If you stop resisting, you will find yourself almost floating towards that old heap of junk. Good. There the rummy is, as expected, passed out under those filthy boxes, a bottle almost empty by its side. *The dummy is a trifle. It is nothing.* No, of course you are not going to intentionally hurt the poor rummy-dummy. Though—just in case—make sure that it is bound securely to that rusty pylon before you begin your practice. It is quite unconscious and is oblivious to the tightness of your belt around its wrists. Well, perhaps that is not true. It is rousing after all, making quite a display of hacking and spitting. Look, it is even opening its crazed, bloodshot eyes to gaze upon you. "Maybe I shouldn't a had that last bottle," the dumb-bummy mutters. Don't you think it almost looks real? Now simply stare at the rummy. Gently clear your mind of all thought and stare without blinking at this mad old thing tied up in front of you. As you consider its perfectly still form, your eyes may burn; your pulse rate may increase—an unpleasant feeling that you are getting too little air—a squeezing sensation up and down your torso as if something is twisting inside. You may imagine you hear something like static or even the roar of an airliner. You may feel lightheaded, like you are going to pass out. Ignore these feelings. They are normal. Now repeat, *"Let me put you together,"* out loud a few times. It is amazing how easy it is and how quickly it all begins. Who knew human limbs could be rearranged like that or that human skin could be so flexible? And look: once its bones are quite gone, doesn't the old rummy-dummy look rather like a slowly melting bar of dirty butter?

STEP 18
"You did it"

Now that you are all done with what passes for a rummy-dummy and now that you have more or less recovered from STEP 17, it is time to set your sights on the skies. Simply look up and wait. There it is now: a large airliner descending some thousands of feet above you, landing gear locking into place. You cannot help yourself, can you? That's right. Just stare at it. Raise that trembling arm. Visualize your arm becoming a crimson mass of spiraling, twitching cords shooting up towards the sky—towards the jet. Watch the emptying mechanism of the aircraft as it comes apart. Watch as the many animal-dummies within are put together—melting flesh with steel and plastic, rearranging and fusing. Witness the airliner-thing's sudden, unnaturally steep and speedy descent into the city's skyline just beyond your sight. Then, some moments later, listen to the tremendous concussion followed by the roar of muffled static beyond the horizon. You did it. You pushed the lever that pulled the cord that made an airliner go down. What a bad boy you are.

STEP 19
"Ultimate Ventriloquism"

The early ventriloquists or gastromancers, literally gut-diviners, were priests—mostly ancient-world hucksters who fooled the ignorant masses into thinking the hollow dummy-idol next to them was speaking with the voice of a god. But every now and again down through the ages, a special kind of ventriloquist-animal-dummy has fallen upon the secret of the only *true* god—the *Ultimate Ventriloquist*—by staring a little too long at a reflection or image of itself—unlocking secrets which in fact can *only* be discovered through the careful, diligent practice of lesser and then Greater Ventriloquism, which leads inexorably to extreme dummy manipulation through the miracle of the Ultimate Ventriloquist, that mysterious archon of manipulation and hollowing. It has so many names, and, truly, no name at all. Now it is time for the most challenging STEP of all but certainly the one that feels the most natural—the most automatic. Cut into your left wrist with a jagged bit of something convenient. Do not resist. Just remember the warning from STEP 9 ("They are all dummies"): turning back is not an option you can exercise at this point. Really open that wrist up. Now, begin to dissect your left arm. There is no need to be careful about it. Search methodically for the cords and the dummy mechanisms inside your arm. Continue the dissection. You may scream. Your pulse rate may race—an excruciating feeling that you are getting too little air—a squeezing sensation throughout your body as if something is twisting its way out. You may begin to imagine you hear something that sounds like static or even the roar of an airliner. You may feel lightheaded like you are going to pass out. Ignore these feelings. They are normal. Now look at what you have found—look into the mirror at yourself one final time. See the twisting, pulsating, intricately connected, pulpy limbs within your limbs—not only inside but like a great, living web *behind* and *around* you. See the bloody cords for what they are now. See that which twitches and pulsates within and outside of torn, translucent flesh. Understand: *the throbbing red pulp within and around you is nothing but the barest trifle of the blackness of those horrible cords and pulleys and levers and stitches that hold the universe together*—you and your dummy and all those hapless, ignorant animal-dummies out there. Yes, you are certainly learning this final STEP the hard way. But, then, that is the only way anyone can ever learn it. All those years yearning for control—ultimate control—over your life and the animal-dummies in it have led to this final moment of surrender. And as you are finally becoming yourself—as the Ultimate Ventriloquist finds a way to speak through you at last—feel its intangible, alien voice twisting through that throat and that mouth, telling us that you have only ever been one of its myriad, crimson arms. Every moment those bloody limbs that are not your limbs become stiffer and colder and that buzzing mind that is not your mind tries to empty itself of the nonsense of sanity and static it has been full of for too long. *You are a trifle. You are nothing.* Feel that voice that is not a voice bubbling through that mouth that is not a mouth. Let it purge you of your static. Let it fill you with its *own* static. Now speak in the language of the Ultimate Ventriloquist—that high pitched, hideous glossolalia worming its way up through those exposed, dead lungs and those exposed, dead vocal cords. You did it. You have found your "dummy voice," which is indeed *nothing* like the voice you once recognized as your own. And as those shrieks mount in volume and intensity, *feel* the presence of the Ultimate Ventriloquist with a body that is not a body and *meditate* on the presence of the Ultimate Ventriloquist with a mind that is not a mind.

STEP 20

We Greater Ventriloquists are acolytes of the Ultimate Ventriloquist. We Greater Ventriloquists are catatonics, emptied of illusions of selfhood and identity. We Greater Ventriloquists no longer toil in any physical way. We think nothing and do nothing. But we Greater Ventriloquists are active. We are active as nature moves us to be: perfect receivers and transmitters of nothing with nothing to stifle the voice of our perfect suffering. Yes, we Greater Ventriloquists speak with the voice of nature making itself suffer. Nothing could be more normal than that. This head is a useless mechanism. Cast it aside. We do not need it anymore. There is nothing but the voice of this pain and this panic thrown into the darkness. It all starts when someone like you begins to suspect that everything is a *trifle*. When someone like you looks at itself in a mirror too long. When someone like you melts the flesh of a street bum into a quivering puddle on the pavement. When someone like you brings a plane down. When someone like you reads these 20 simple steps to ventriloquism. When someone like you is put together. When someone like you is put together. When someone like you is put together.

The Infusorium

"They were firing up for the grade and the smoke was belching out, but it didn't rise. I mean it didn't go up at all. It just spilled out over the lip of the stack like a black liquid, like ink or oil, and rolled down to the ground and lay there. My God, it just lay there!"

—Berton Roueché, "The Fog," *The New Yorker*, 1950

- 1 -

At first I couldn't get the fucking skull to stop screaming no matter what I did.

But you don't want to hear about that.

You want to know why I killed him.

- 2 -

I was on my way to the university library. The fog had gone from yellowish to brownish, and visibility had fallen to about twenty yards in any direction. It was the first chill air of the season, but it was *stagnant* air—oppressive, smelly smog that stung my eyes and produced many sneezing and wheezing fits. Lucky me, I'm asthmatic and had already gone through about five puffs of my inhaler that morning with diminishing returns.

The night before, the local weatherman described the atmospheric condition in Dunnstown as being "...like putting a lit cigarette in a bowl then placing a blanket on top of that. The smoke has no way of escaping." Paper mill days, we call them, when the factories north of town bring the omnipresent smell of farts among us. On those days, a dark fishbowl haze shrouds the city. A lit cigarette in a bowl. Good description. Made me want to light up. I guess smoking two packs a day on top of everything else didn't help my asthma, but that's a different story.

Once in the library, I remembered how much I hated them. The musty stench. The tense, forced silence. And especially the librarians themselves—mostly old, testy bats and coots. I'm not talking about the young library assistants and other cart pushers they have working there. I mean the self-important bozos who run the place.

As I walked through the sliding glass doors, I approached one such bug-eyed geezer at the circulation desk.

"Detective Tosto, Dunnstown PD," I said, flashing my badge.

Bug-eyes stared at me as if he'd never seen a female cop before. Asked me what my business was with a shitty little sneer on his face. Yeah, librarians like bug-eyes burn my ass.

"Need some help researching a local crime scene. Do I need to talk to your boss?"

Bug-eyes flinched and referred me to the reference department. Specifically to Mr. Solomon Kroth, a tall man with a fancy mane of gray hair and a lean, serious face of the kind I favor. He and I recognized early on that we were both outsiders. Had a nice back and forth about the Deep South, the city of Dunnstown in particular, and back-asswards residents like my partner. Unlike bug-eyes, Kroth was friendly—enthusiastic even. Unusual in a librarian, at least in my experience.

I asked him about Treasure Forest. Beaming, he directed me to the second floor to Collections and the Government Serials department, where I would find old periodicals and copies of city archives. A lot of what I read about up there mentioned a lone paper mill in the area I was interested in. It was a pretty old factory. Built in the mid-nineteenth century. It transitioned to printing press and back to pulp mill in the early twentieth century. The city condemned the factory in the 50s when twenty workers and half as many townsfolk died in a little known environmental clusterfuck. And there the defunct factory complex still stands in that smoldering fishbowl, Treasure Forest, in the middle of what is now Dunnstown's Municipal Park.

After several hours, I went back downstairs to the Reference department and asked Kroth what he knew about the old mill. He retrieved a few overhead photos of the place to show me, pointing out that the vegetation in the area didn't seem to touch the factory.

"Another interesting fact about the mill grounds," Kroth said. "Treasure Forest typically has a kind of lingering smoke that clings to the ground, even on clear days. And visible particulate matter."

"Yeah," I replied. "I've seen it. Heard the City of Dunnstown has a controlled fire going on nearby to clear brush."

"Oh yuh-yes. That's what they say. Huh-huh-here's where the matter becomes even more interesting. There's actually evidence I found in several old local periodicals that the Treasure Forest area has been inundated with this atmospheric effect for decades. The smoke is, I believe, duh-due to some kind of lingering, toxic effect of the old factory's presence."

It was cute how the librarian started to stutter and kind of hopped when he got enthusiastic. It was clear that Treasure Forest and this mill really floated Kroth's boat. Fun for him. Helpful (and amusing) for me.

"Detective Tosto, would you mind stepping into my office?" Kroth asked, leading me into a large, glorified cubicle.

"Please, call me Raph. Everyone does." Thought the fucker was about to ask me out to dinner, and I was inclined to take him up on the offer.

"Ah, yes. Puh-please sit. Tell me, detective, what is your interest in Treasure Forest and the mill within it?"

"Probably nothing. Just part of a little case I've been working on," I said, reclining on a squeaky, time worn chair. That's when I noticed the odd illustration pinned above Kroth's workstation. It consisted of a white tree on a black background—the upper half with leafy growth and the bottom half entwined with skeletal roots. There were a series of circles superimposed within the upper and lower halves of the tree. Nine above, two that intersected each other in the middle, and nine below.

"What's that?" I asked.

"Oh," Kroth said with a sparkle in his eye, "That, detective, is the Tree of Life and Death. From the Qabalah. Jewish mysticism, you know. What interests me most is the lower portion of the piece, the Qliphothic Tree of Death... or puh-perhaps *False-Life* would be a better description. After all, Qliphoth luh-literally means 'husk' or 'shell.' As above, so below. Growth even in death, and yet the life or, rather, the appearance of life is mirrored by its distorted image underground. As above, so buh-below. Please, take it, detective." Pulling the illustration down, he placed it in front of me. "For inspiration. Excuse me."

Then Kroth pulled out a mottled, greenish steel oxygen tank from under his desk. He placed the tank's black, opaque mask over his head—covering his nose and mouth—turned its squeaking valve and breathed deeply for what felt like ten minutes. Then he twisted the valve closed and replaced mask and tank back under his desk.

"Apologies," the librarian said. "I also kuh-keep a clean, extra shirt and jacket at work during this season. You see, this time of year I find by midday my original ones have become quite dingy. Clothing can be changed. Lungs, sadly, cannot. I am afraid the particulates in the atmosphere have done vuh-vile work on my whole system, causing no end of physical troubles. Coughing fits, shuh-shortness of breath. The worst biological changes. For instance, you do nuh-know the blood of the non-killed pollutant victim is literally *thicker*, don't you?"

Kroth lost me there. I just stared in response.

"Ahem," the librarian said. I think it's the first time I ever heard someone literally say that word. Too bad. I was beginning to hate this guy.

"Look, I'm running a little short on time, Solomon."

"Please, if you don't mind, I puh-prefer 'Mr. Kroth.'"

I snorted in response. Yeah, no way was this stuttering, self-important prick getting a date, let alone getting into my pants.

"Back to the matter at hand, then," Kroth said. "The old mill and your, heh, 'luh-little case.' It's a small suh-suh-city, detective. The word on the street, as they say—at least in certain quarters—is out ruh-regarding the oddly appendaged, skeletal corpses found buried in Treasure Forest, even if the luh-local media is still ignorant of them. Tuh-tell me, what makes you think the old mill has anything to duh-duh-do with them?"

Librarian guy was now jiggling like a bunny rabbit afire, but it no longer seemed so cute to me. He had my full attention, though. Kroth had used the word "appendaged," and that definitely rang a bell.

"Well," I replied, "Proximity for one. Whoever skeletonized those bodies would need some place to work. Somewhere isolated. Tell me, Mr. Kroth, you ever been out to Treasure Forest yourself, maybe in the mill area?"

My question sent the librarian into a sudden coughing and wheezing fit that lasted at least a couple of minutes. When he finally caught his breath he said, "Go up there to the mill? No, nuh-no. Not for many yuh-years. The air quality there is..." He pulled his steel oxygen tank out and was soon huffing oxygen again. After he removed his mask, Kroth sneezed, and the librarian caught his snot with a fancy white, monogrammed handkerchief. I noticed its surface had become mottled with what looked like runny soot.

"That area is positively ruh-ruh-wretched with particulate matter. And duh-dangerous for other reasons as well. For uh-instance, I happen to have direct evidence that the Factory wuh-was also connected to the tragic crash of Dunntown's Pan Am Flight 389."

"Wait, the Factory was somehow connected to a plane crash here in Dunnstown? When?"

"Indeed. One of the worst airplane duh-disasters in US history. Long before your time here. As the puh-puh-plane was about to land, it crashed into what was then the St. Peters public housing project on Tanner Williams Road. Not a mile from the old Factory. Killed all 285 passengers aboard. Cuh-created a dense fireball that consumed several populated street blocks. It's tuh-tuh-true. It was just awful. Surprised you haven't heard of it before, Detective. It's a vuh-very famous airplane accident."

"Yeah, well, I hate plane travel, and personally I don't get my jollies obsessing over mass fucking deaths."

"Puh-please," Kroth said, with an index finger extended towards me, "Language."

I snorted.

"There was," he proclaimed (no other word for it), "a connection to a man who was living in the abandoned factory at the time. His name was Joseph Snavely, author of this manuscript here."

He handed me a small, rather crushed looking chapbook.

"20 Simple Steps to Ventriloquism?" I said, reading the title. Looked like it had been printed using a typewriter on the verge of giving up the ghost.

"Indeed. That puh-plane crash was Snavely's doing, you see, at luh-least in some sense. It's curious you've come in now, detective, buh-buh-because I've only just begun lobbying the federal authorities about the issue. My ruh-research indicates..."

"Hold the boat, Kraft."

"Kroth," he replied indignantly. *Indignantly!*

"Whatever. Are you saying that this Snavely guy—this, uh, ventriloquist slash homeless guy—was some kind of domestic terrorist?"

"Not quite, Detective. But I assure you he was no mere lesser ventriloquist. Mr. Snavely was a guh-Greater ventriloquist."

The capital "G" was implied.

"Greater ventriloquist?" I replied. "They come in different sizes?"

Librarian guy didn't even crack a smile.

The next fifteen minutes were spent pulling myself away from the pushy and—my guess was—batshit crazy Solomon Kroth. He warned me against investigating Treasure Forest, let alone the old factory. He also pushed the "20 Simple Steps to Ventriloquism" manual into my hands and insisted that I give it a careful read as soon as I could. Flipping through it quickly, I was starting to think that Kroth himself was the author of the piece.

In the end, Mr. Solomon Kroth did indeed ask me to dinner "to discuss the muh-matter further."

I snorted again and replied with a "Yeah, that's not happening... *Sol.*"

When I made my way through the stinking aquarium of fog back to the cruiser, Guidry appeared. He was leaning against a nearby pine tree, stuffing his fat face with a cheeseburger, grinning—talking up some clueless co-ed.

"So, how did it go, Raph? Learn anything?" Guidry asked with his mouth full.

"Sure," I said, crumpling up the occult illustration and tossing it and the manual into the cruiser's trunk. "Oh, and I remembered something too. I hate librarians."

"Pfft. Big surprise, Raphie. You hate everyone."

- 3 -

Detective Michael Thomas Guidry and I had been partners for the better part of three years—not long after I moved down to Dunnstown after all the ugliness up north. We made kind of an unusual pairing, especially in a small city in the ass end of Alabama. See, big surprise, but there aren't many female detectives on the force down here—let alone in Homicide.

Guidry, though, he was a strange bird. You've probably never heard that about him, but he was. People liked Guidry. He was good with them. I liked Guidry too. Hell, I *loved* him. No, don't give me that smirk. I'll let you in on a secret that'll contradict everything else you've heard about the two of us. Guidry and I were never a thing. Yeah, Yeah. I know everyone thinks we were. Always did, even before all the shit went down. But I never even kissed the guy. Not on the mouth or anywhere else. Christ no. Guidry was chock-full of what they call boyish charm. And I find boyish charm repulsive—at least sexually.

But you want to know about the case, not my turn offs. I heard about the skeletons for the first time about a week after I moved to Dunnstown, brand new on the force. Seemed that every year—usually around mid-fall at the foggy, farty height of the paper mill days—the Dunnstown second police district received duplicates of the following letter:

> To Whom It May Concern,
>
> As a longtime resident of Dunnstown, I wish to express my concern at the expansive decrepitude that has infected the Municipal Park area. What was once largely a benign manifestation has become a malignant one. People are disappearing in this city—more of them every year. The elderly, the sick, the very young. The victims vanish on the darkest paper mill days and nights. These unfortunates are no longer alive in any normal sense. Their bodies have undergone a garish array of mutations. I do not understand the process they endured (or, perhaps, continue to endure), but I

will describe their skeletonized remains from a visual perspective:

1) Color, black.
2) Skulls, normal. Visibly Homo Sapien.
3) Heavy.
4) Limbs *elongated*. Far too many joints. Hands and feet altered in a mockery of natural ones, appendaged like sea creatures or insects.
5) Corpses measure between seven to twelve feet in length and three to five feet in width.
6) Like an explosion from inside out, frozen in time. But all corpses intact, contained within their twisted forms.

I have discovered where the victims are being taken and where their remains are interred. You may find them buried in Municipal Park, Treasure Forest area. Action must be taken before the next slew of paper mill days. Conditions will worsen. I suspect the corpses themselves are contagious. Protect yourselves.

Signed,
Anonymous

This had gone on every year for the past ten or so. Of course, no missing persons had been reported, so it was considered a hoax. You might imagine how these letters played in the DPD. Around Halloween each year, the guys in Homicide—ever mature and sophisticated gents—spent a great deal of time "borrowing" plaster skeletons from various schools about town. They painted them black and attached ridiculous implements in place of extra limbs. These modified pseudo-skeletons were then placed strategically around the station. They'd use them to shock rookies or otherwise skittish detectives. Boo! A skeleton falls out of a closet. Boo! A skeleton pops up from under a desk. And then, man, would their fellow veteran-compatriots guffaw. Those dead-eyed good ol' boys sure enjoyed their hi-larious pranks ("You been skeletonized!" they'd yell at their victims).

But when they tried to shock little-ole-Yankee-ingénue-detective-me with one of those plaster skeleton jobbies? Well, one morning I opened the door to the armory, and one of those things sprung out of the darkness of the room at me. Without a screech or a flinch, I broke the thing in half. Everyone was real pissed about it. Except Guidry, of course. He just giggled and proceeded to take me under his sizable wing. He'd lost his own partner to retirement the year before and was able to pull some strings to make me his new bud-in-crime-fighting.

Of course, even with Guidry as my partner, the others never accepted me as one of the fold. I was on the outside with everyone but Guidry. Which, of course, was more than fine by me. As for Guidry, I thought at first he just wanted in my pants, but he seemed about as physically attracted to me as I was to him. Believe it or not, I always appreciated that about Guidry. He just liked me. And, as silly as the man was (or maybe because of that), the feeling was mutual.

So, the skeletons—the *real* skeletons. This past fall, my third in Dunnstown, ten Dunnstowners were reported missing for the first time. It was around the same time that we received our latest annual letter. Every damn one of the missing persons was a peculiar range of elderly and/or otherwise sickly folks. Last seen within the area in and around Municipal Park.

Who bothered to do the thirty minutes of research it took to recognize the link between the letters and the disappearances? Me. Suddenly, our anonymous letter writer was a potential suspect—maybe for kidnapping, maybe for worse. Yearly hi-larious skeleton prank ritual ruined by yours truly. Yeah, I sure was Ms. Popularity with my peers.

Not long afterwards, Guidry and I geared up and led a small group, combing Municipal Park for the bodies. And—boom—in short order we had our skeletons. Guidry came upon the first one by accident as he strolled down a fog-soaked Treasure Forest path. I remember him waddling ahead of me, grinning up at the smoky silhouettes of scorched, rail thin pine trees as if they were anything worth looking at. Suddenly, he fell flat on his huge belly, giggling, leaving me shaking my head and rolling my eyes in semi-irritated bemusement. When he got up at last, sweeping away the smoky crud that clung to the ground, he and I saw the thing more or less at the same time. Shrouded in a bed of discolored pine straw was a blackened human skull embedded face up.

"Oh man," said Guidry, in his south Alabama drawl. "Just like *Motel Hell*. Ever see that one, Raph?"

Yeah, that was my Guidry: ever good-natured, even when it was unnatural to be.

We found seven more bodies in the same position—buried feet first in the ground, skull-faces just above the soil. As the letters had indicated, the skeletons' resemblance to human ones began and ended with the skulls themselves. The blackened skeletal remains gave the impression they had expanded below the dirt, outwards and downwards. And everything about the skeletons underground was *elongated*. Limbs, digits, even ribs and backbone just as described, terminating in crablike claws or the jointed, thin legs of an insect. Average length, twelve feet. Average width, seven feet. Just as Mr. Anonymous letter guy had described to the department for ten years running.

I didn't like touching those scummy things, even with the gloves. No one did. The bones were a deep black color inside and out and were heavier than they should've been by half. It was for this reason that I didn't think at first they were authentic bones at all. My first thought was that they were maybe composite pieces of metal welded together by a talented but whacked out local artist. This was, of course, before Forensics later verified that the skin, blood and organs found within the marrow of each skeleton were in fact consistent with individual—not composite—human bodies. DNA evidence also eventually ID'd four of our ten missing persons among the corpses. In those first couple of days, though, I was half convinced that the Dunnstown Police Department was the victim of another hi-larious "skeletonizing" hoax.

At any rate, it was clear that our letter writer knew his (or her) stuff when it came to these bodies. After my recent library visit with Kroth, I reviewed my notes and the most recent missive from our serial letter writer and compared. "Hands and feet altered in a mockery of natural ones, appendaged like sea creatures or insects." *Appendaged?* Not a term I'd ever heard... except from the stuttering mouth of a certain librarian. Yeah, I'd be having more words with

Mr. Solomon Kroth. But first things first.

"Guidry," I said. "We're headed back to Treasure Forest tomorrow morning."

"Sure thing, boss."

My partner seemed as carefree and jovial about taking on this bizarre, gruesome case as he ever did about anything. Nothing much got to friend Guidry—till the day we investigated the factory.

I realized early the night before we went out to the park that I couldn't smoke a cigarette without coughing till I almost puked. Later learned that pretty much all Dunnstown smokers quit temporarily that evening. Cigarettes of any brand suddenly tasted like rotten plums.

The next day, even foggier and more putrid than the last, Guidry and I headed out to the abandoned mill.

There's something so ill conceived about Municipal Park. It's not that it isn't well maintained. Most of it is. But the park kind of goes on and on, you know? It's *merged* with that part of town in a way, and I'm still not clear where the park ends and where the rest of the city begins. It doesn't help that Dunnstown is subject to these thick, putrid fogs that last day and night. But even when the sky is clear I can't tell Municipal Park from the rest of the neighborhoods around it.

Example: heading towards downtown, once you get beyond the big ditch-waterfall thing, past the dingy old train, the "I Dream of Jeannie" looking jet and the big, green, peeling archway entrance to the park, you realize you're in a conventional green space and, simultaneously, in a suburb of the shitty, dilapidated, ranch-style house variety. And you wonder, "Are these people living *in* the park or just on its borders?" Then you notice Bronco Billy's—a crappy little bar that's been there from time immemorial—kind of tucked between the rental boat place and a ravaged looking set of swings. Man, how is that even legal? Just a quick turn around the corner and you're in the park proper, with the city museum on your right and all the ducks and geese again behind it. But then just a bit up the road across the street there's an old Naval recruiting station. Has this huge parking lot that I've never seen more than a couple of cars parked in. And up the hill from that—more of the ranch-style, single story monstrosities. Followed by Treasure Forest.

Have you actually been out to Treasure Forest? Dunnstown Botanical Gardens sits somewhere in there along with what's left of the paper mill. It's a pretty wooded area. But have you noticed how the underbrush is kind of wasting away? The vines and the branches all yellowed? Those ugly, skinny, pine straw-making machines are all scorched about a foot or two above their roots. On paper mill days or clear ones, a kind of smoke or smog clings to the ground, just as Kroth mentioned. Sometimes gives the impression that you're walking on top of a greasy thunderhead or a steaming, scummy pond.

Guidry and I stopped and made the short hike through Treasure Forest, up a steep hill, and there in a clearing stood the old mill. It's not a pretty building, and I can't imagine it ever was. Dark green. Shit green. I think it's rectangular, but it's hard to say from the limited visibility.

The first time we visited the factory, Guidry and I explored the grounds as well as we could in the crap fog. It's like you're out in the country but without the birds singing and squirrels and shit. None of that. Almost underwater quiet. Kroth had been right about the air quality—it stinks in general but especially around the mill. Little black or gray bits of what Guidry called ash floated in the brownish murk. Whatever it was in the air set my asthma right off. Two albuterol puffs. Three. Guidry didn't seem to notice or much care. He could've been on vacation.

"Damn," I said, observing the petrified looking bushes and vines all around the mill. Nut job Kroth had been right about that too. While the flora looked like shit in Treasure Forest, here around the derelict factory it was brown and brittle with old death. Just as if the mill had poisoned the good goddamn earth all around it.

The corroded metal door of the central building stood ajar, and somewhere unseen above us, I knew, hung the factory's inert smokestack.

The air quality was worse inside than it had been outside, filled with fog or smoke or some unpleasant combination of them all. There was, of course, no power in the building. We entered the rectangular, nondescript lobby, with its half exposed, stone walls and old, rotten boards. Visibility was nil.

I shambled back to the cruiser, sneezing and hacking, to retrieve a couple of surgical-looking filter masks, a pair of protective goggles and two flashlights. Kroth's warnings and our previous experience with the skeleton digs had prepped us to bring that sort of gear.

"Nice," Guidry said after we donned masks and goggles and switched on our flashlights. "You look like you just stepped right out of *The Road Warrior!*"

"Shut it. If you're right about the serial killer thing our man could be in there right now."

"Or our girl. Ooh! A lady artist serial killer."

"Ladies first." With that I beckoned him to enter the mill ahead of me.

Happy go lucky Guidry just giggled, his ample belly jiggling as it always did. Now you follow why I never fucked him?

So we went through one of the two doors on either side of the mill lobby and the adjacent office that led into the mill proper. We explored several large rooms at length, all filled with equipment I recognized from my library research—the bottom part of a rusty old digester, dripping storage tanks, and tons of pipes running up and down and all around us.

"Sweet Jesus, Guidry, look at all the junk floating in the air. Is this goddamn mill operational?"

Because what looked like the ashes floating outside and inside the lobby were also floating around the mill house itself. An even denser whatever it was—at least in our flashlights' beams.

"No way, but that's pretty weird stuff all right," Guidry replied. "Y'know, it almost looks like one of those Christmas globes with gray or black instead of white snow floating around, don't it?"

"Well, that shit better not be asbestos drifting down from the ceiling and walls," I replied, checking out a couple of small, single stall restrooms with matching toilets (complete with matching, petrified shit in the bowls). "Ugh. If I get asbestosis or something one day because of this, I'll kill you, Guidry."

"But you know what this stuff really reminds me of, Raphie? Sea Monkeys."

"Sea Monkeys? Am I supposed to know what that means? This isn't the setup for some stupid redneck joke, is it?"

Guidry giggled. "*Sea Monkeys.* They were a real thing years back, though maybe a little before your time. Used to advertise in that old Boy Scout magazine, *Boy's Life.*"

"Jesus, I don't want to hear about this, Guidry. Boy Scouts? Pfft. No way you were a Boy Scout. For Christ's sake..."

"Only made Cub Scout," Guidry replied as he searched down row after row of giant paper spools. "Anywho, the advertisement had this family of undersea people with webbed hands, gills, the works. I think there were a little king and a queen and a couple of kids. Sea Monkeys in an aquarium inside a castle with this big ol' kid's face staring in at them."

"Wow. You're old. With the maturity of a third grader." I paused for a deep-throated, hacking cough. "You know what, bud, can you speed it up? I'd kind of like to finish with this before suppertime. Ack. Not that I'm likely to eat much."

"Sure, sure, Raphie. The point is I saved up my allowance when I was about ten and bought the thing. Came with a miniature, red plastic aquarium covered in these magnifying circles. Had packets full of, what, eggs? Fish food? Both? Fill up the things with water, pour the powder in, and in a few days—kaboom!—Sea Monkeys."

"So did they end up looking like a miniature royal family from the Black Lagoon?"

"Well, no. In a few days, I saw little white specks squirming around the tank—maybe a dozen of em. I was let down at how they turned out. No hands or legs or cute little faces like in the ad. Later found out they were a type of miniature shrimp, but what the Sea Monkeys really looked like—well—the closest I can come to describing em is, uh, sperm."

"Oh, God, here we go. I spent all this time listening to your boring ass story only to be sexually harassed?"

"Naw, naw," Guidry replied, giggle-cackling and half-ass-inspecting the sidelights in what appeared to be a ruined storage room. "Really. They looked just like oversized sperm, kind of jerking around the little tank. They were just rubbery little things like you'd expect to see in some kind of state fair ride or something. I was into em for a day or two after that. Put em on the far side of my bed. I think some Sea Monkey food came with the kit, and, uh, I somehow forgot to feed them."

"Ugh. As soon as we get out of here I'm contacting PETA."

Guidry giggled. "My point is this—when I remembered to check on em about a week or so later, what was left of em was just floating around, suspended in the dirty water. Through the magnifying lenses I could see em though, and I couldn't believe how skeletal they looked. Like I could see tiny ribs and other bones if I looked real close. I kept em for a long time—just... I couldn't stop watching those little Sea Monkey bodies. Looked more like real little things dead than they ever did when they were alive."

"Ok, now you're repulsing me, Guidry. Stop. I already feel like throwing up."

"And, anyway, this stuff in the air in here and outside for that matter, it reminds me of them Sea Monkey bodies. Just thought I'd share that," he said, grinning through his mask, squinting and jiggling with laughter.

"Thanks, doofus." I said. "Go around to the left and I'll hit the right side."

So we finished sweeping through the front half of the mill. I knew the small doors on either side of us just ahead could access the wood yard.

I walked down near one of them when Guidry waved me over. He was near a small compartment I hadn't noticed, fumbling with its handle.

"What are you doing, dumbo?" I asked, "Don't you think we should search the wood yard before you start dicking with electrical boxes?"

"This ain't an electrical box, Raphie," Guidry replied. He opened the metal panel, which gave a rusty-hinged shriek, revealing a long enclosed compartment. It housed a ladder, blackened with grime.

"Jesus, smells like the paper mill shit itself and died up there." I said, gagging.

"Mmmm. Smells like money to me," Guidry replied, giggling.

"Crummy. Ladies first," I said with a bow, as he entered in front of me.

After that, it was clink, clink, clink up into the darkness, the flashlight beams filled with Guidry's Sea Monkey skeletons in my imagination. We entered an open balcony area overlooking the pulp mill below us, not that we could see much thanks to the bad lighting and all the goddamn ashes in the air. Along the front wall I saw some large, blacked out windows over a series of huge standing closets. A hardware shop. On the far side of the balcony space, a door led to a cube-shaped control booth (with ancient wiring and rusted crank-like levers still intact).

Then I heard a clicking noise behind me and turned around, squatting like one of Charlie's Angels with my gun out.

"Over there," Guidry whispered. "I thought I saw a face for a second."

Another echoing click in the smoky darkness. And then another.

"What's that? A pipe?" I whispered.

"No way. There ain't been a working pipe here for at least thirty years. Wait here."

"Fuck that. I'm coming with you."

He turned back towards me then with his masked face and his index finger held up over where his mouth would be. His belly quivered in a soundless giggle. Of course he was enjoying this. I gave him my own finger in turn and followed him into a kind of grid of metal and plywood running over the pulp mill below—a makeshift way to get at the pipes that crisscrossed in every direction.

The thin flooring creaked and the ceiling hung low—no more than three feet above us. I banged my head with a curse more than once on the overhanging piping which swept in front of us now and again. Every five feet or so, there appeared a triangular opening where another series of black pipes hung over the pulp mill below. The clicking continued getting louder and louder, but I couldn't pick up any pattern to it. Just a hollow kind of tap. Pause. Tap. Pause pause. Tap.

I saw the body out of the corner of my eye before Guidry did — child-size, hung halfway over one of the gaps in the grid, close to falling down to the mill house floor. Without a second thought, I lunged for it, promptly whacking my head on one of those invisible pipes in the process, this time hard enough to make me see stars. I staggered backwards and landed on my ass. Guidry ambled by me, and by the time I recovered he was holding—cradled like a baby—a small skeleton.

"What the fuck, Guidry? What the *fuck*?"

Guidry just stared at me through his goggles. I turned my flashlight beam—wavy with those black, floating motes—onto the body. Something like the skeletons we had dug up recently. But far more hideous than any of them. It appeared to be fresher. The remains of the thing's yellowed, shriveled skin cracked across its face like desiccated sand. Its mouth hung open to reveal a single line of small, dark teeth. The hair was black and slick, almost as if painted high on its head, giving the illusion of premature balding.

Below the neck the child-thing seemed more insect than human. Too many arms, or were they legs? Whatever the case, they were far too long and jointed. I had no idea how Guidry could bring himself to touch the thing, let alone cuddle up to it. But worst of all, the thing's eyes—its great, round googly eyes. I've never seen eyes like that on a human being. The eyes of a doll, of a shark—still intact in its head.

"My god, Raph. Just a kid."

"Not sure that was a kid, Guidry. Just put it down."

"They told us this wouldn't happen."

As if in response, the thing's mouth shut with a loud click. I let out a bark, and my partner threw the body down.

A nasty crack rang out as the child-thing smacked one of the pipes, followed by a more distant shattering noise about thirty feet below. Guidry stumbled forward, though I managed to break his fall, preventing him from slumping over into the triangular wedge of darkness.

We breathed hard and coughed and sweated, tangled up together for a while, and then I managed to heave Guidry to his feet.

"What did you say a minute ago?" I asked. "'They' said what?"

Guidry didn't respond. His balding head shone with sweat. He stripped off both goggles and mask.

"Oh God, Raphie, I think I broke him." He turned and waddled out of the pipe grid, coughing.

"Broke what? That kid-thing? Was that even human? The fuck, Guidry?"

But he didn't respond, staggering into the control room and back towards the ladder. I followed, clutching my still tender head.

"Where the hell are you going, Guidry?"

"I got to make sure he ain't broken."

"Are you out of your goddamn mind? That thing's way past breaking." I caught up with Guidry and turned him around, grasping him by his meaty shoulders. "Look, it's almost five thirty, and that whatever it is isn't going anywhere. Anyway, we'll need backup before we come back."

Pale and shivering, he let me lead him down the ladder and drag him out of the factory, down the hill to the twilit grove below it and into the passenger side of the cruiser. I drove maybe a half a mile down the winding road past the Naval Recruiting station when I had to stop for Guidry to puke. Then I puked, too. We had that black and gray gunk all over us from head to foot, though Guidry had gotten by far the worst of it. He had breathed in all that shit sans mask and couldn't stop coughing for a long while after upchucking.

Later, on the way out of Municipal Park, I started in on Guidry.

"So, you care to explain what you said back there?" I asked, making sure to take my turns extra slow, both for our stomachs' sakes and because the visibility outside was so poor.

"What?"

"What you told me up there—'they said it wouldn't happen.' Who?"

Guidry just stared in the pseudo-darkness of the cruiser.

"The fuck, Guidry? Who is 'they?'"

Guidry's mouth dropped open, and he glared at me as if I had just asked him if Jesus liked to do it doggy-style.

"You goddamned Dunnstowners," I said, forcing a laugh.

"No, Raph. No. This isn't funny. You weren't there after the 389 crashed. You didn't see what happened."

"Didn't see *what*? What kind of shit are you mixed up in, Mike?" I had never seen him so worked up (or, come to think of it, worked up at all... about anything).

After dropping off Guidry without another word, I popped the cruiser's trunk. Then I pulled out the illustration I had thrown in there the day before—next to the "20 Simple Steps to Ventriloquism" manual. I looked at the Tree of Life and False-Life illustration that Kroth had passed off to me. Flipping the sheet over, I saw a street address scrawled there followed by "drop by when you want to know more" scrawled in spidery letters underneath it. I grabbed the little book too, slammed the trunk and got back into the cruiser. By that point, after being clear of the fucking paper mill air-gunk for a while, my appetite had improved. Looked like Mr. Kroth and I were going to have that dinner date after all.

- 5 -

The "date" didn't happen that evening, though. Fact is, I got lost on my way there thanks to the greasy, gagging fishbowl fog. Ended up sitting in the cruiser on the side of some half-suburb, half-park street all night long, waiting for dawn. In the car's dome light, though, I caught up on my reading. The only thing on hand was Kroth's ventriloquist manual. One of the steps in the book involved "bringing a plane down" through something the ostensible author, Joseph Snavely, called "Greater Ventriloquism." I was shaken up. I kept thinking about Guidry's mention of the plane crash (Flight 389) in connection with something he saw. Something to do with the Factory and maybe the kid-thing too. I slept like shit that night, as you might expect. Dreamt about hybrid spider/ventriloquist dummies, heads twisted backwards, facing up, skidding on top of a kind of lazy river inside a huge greenhouse.

I woke in the semidarkness of morning. Couldn't bring myself to eat a thing, let alone yesterday's half eaten bagel bagged up on the cruiser's floorboard. I had struggled with my asthma all night, waking up over and over again in the back seat with a start, wracked with coughing fits and worse. I'm sure I sucked in far more inhaled steroids into my body that night than was medically safe, but at least I was more or less alive.

Meanwhile, my cop radio was full of business. Many of the townsfolk had developed the same symptoms I had experienced overnight—abdominal pain, nausea and vomiting, splitting headache, choking and shortness of breath, even coughing up blood. By that morning the local clinic had a long line of residents, all in positions of wrack or uneasy repose. Twenty-two people, nineteen of them asthmatics like me, died in the night. The DFD and the DPD were busy scrounging up oxygen tanks for the smog victims. I determined that as soon as I made it to Kroth's house I was also going to take a long draw from whatever oxygen tank he no doubt had squirreled away there.

I figured Kroth would be at home. The fog by that point was so thick that only idiots like me were attempting to drive.

Kroth lived not far from Municipal Park and the university on the far west, semi-rural side of town. Even in the meager light of mid-morning, it took me a couple of hours in that fucking fog, and I still had a couple of minor fender benders along the way. Once at a railway crossing, the cruiser was nearly broadsided by a muted locomotive engine puffing down the tracks. I slammed on the brakes just in time. The train wound its way through the fog-diseased park neighborhood—appearing and disappearing like a ghost of itself. It looked to be an old engine, almost a twin of the rusted one displayed near the park's entrance, its smokestack belching dark billowy fumes. But its smoke didn't rise. It just oozed over the lip of the stack like black ink and collected pond-like on the ground around the cruiser.

Kroth's neighborhood contained the same nauseating houses found all around the park. His was also ranch-style, of course—a red brick jobbie with moldy, yellow siding, but otherwise indistinguishable from the others on his street. I strapped on my Glock, walked to the front door and banged its ornate, cheap looking knocker.

"Who is it?" asked a husky voice that sounded nothing like the librarian I had met just a couple days back. Was this Kroth's lover?

"Detective Tosto, Dunnstown Police," I said in husky response and immediately fell into a coughing fit before croaking, "Is this the residence of Solomon Kroth?"

The porch light turned on, and I heard the deadbolt unlock and the chain rattle. The door opened, and there was Kroth standing before me—or someone like him. The styled, ample gray hair appeared disheveled and damp—the dapper, tweed-jacketed librarian of yesterday now wore a dingy gray wife beater and a pair of blown out jeans that left both of his angular knees poking out. Kroth's feet were bare, and his skin was a light shade of blue.

"Detective Tosto. Stay right there."

After about thirty seconds he returned to the porch holding a pair of tweezers and what appeared to be a test tube.

"What the fuck?" I asked.

"Language, detective."

Kroth plucked something gray from the right side of my head with the tweezers and dropped it into the tube.

"Touch me again, and you'll be gargling your own balls."

"I see you've been to the paper mill in spite of my warnings," he replied, shaking the test tube. "Please come in, detective."

"You look blue, Kroth," I said, following him into a small foyer and then into a living room decorated as if by a Southern Baptist octogenarian. Smelled like it too in spite of the fog-stench.

"Yes, your skin is also cyanotic, a symptom of oxygen deprivation," he replied, gesturing for me to sit on a Victorian style, high-back couch. The couch, the two chairs (also of the high-backed, Victorian variety), and in fact, every piece of the uncomfortable looking furniture in the room was swathed in transparent, plastic sheeting. And, upon closer inspection, the walls right to the ceiling were covered as well.

"You planning to kill someone today or are you just that obsessive?"

Kroth ignored my question and pulled out a twin of the oxygen tank I had seen a couple of days before in the library.

"Please sit and put this mask over your face before you fall down." he said, and I did. Soon I was sucking oxygen and feeling sweet relief. I de-masked, and Kroth wheeled the tank away.

"What happened to you, detective?" he asked. "Tell me all."

So I told Kroth what happened yesterday in the mill.

"Okay," I said after I finished. "Question: any idea who 'they' are? The ones Guidry mentioned?"

Kroth sighed, rubbing his puffy eyes and slumping in an ornate chair next to a miniature organ. There wasn't a hint of the jumpy, stuttering librarian from a couple of days back. In fact, this guy looked like he was about to eat the barrel of a pistol at any second.

"Do you really want to know?" he asked.

"Yeah, and I'd also like to know what *your* interest is in all this, Kroth. Why the stuttering, nutty, bouncy act the other day when I asked about Treasure Forest and the mill?"

"That was no act, detective. I am the victim of an unfortunate nervous condition. My ailment, exacerbated by these wretched paper mill days, often drives me to highs of a narcissistic nature. As evidenced by my behavior at work two days ago. It's beyond my control—as is my current depressive state, also brought on by this week's weather. The paper mill days have gone on too long this year. Too long."

"Look, Sol, I'm not your shrink. I'd just like to know what's going on in Treasure goddamn Forest."

"Which part of what's going on, detective?" Kroth asked, expressionless. "The constant, controlled burning in Treasure Forest or the ashes floating outside and inside of the abandoned mill? The mystery of Joseph Snavely, and the horror his ventriloquism wrought on Dunnstown? Or the reason why its denizens are disappearing one by one, more every year, only to reappear as deformed skeletons buried in Treasure Forest. Or perhaps you would like to know about the skeleton-dummy you found hanging over a ceiling pipe in the old factory."

My right hand moved under my jacket, and I unholstered my gun.

"Now now, before you arrest me for a crime I did not commit, Detective Tosto, I will relay just what you likely think you most want to know."

"I was right," I said, "You're the letter writer."

"Yes, yes, of course I wrote those letters, every year for the past ten. In my manic state, I still imagined such efforts would make a difference, and I was correct. Those letters of mine made things far worse, and things will get worse still for all of us. Would you like to know the genesis of Dunnstown's problems and my nervous condition, detective? Read the manual I gave you. Ask your police chief. Ask the Brotherhood of the Black Fog. Ask what it is they serve."

I had pulled my firearm out but held it, barrel-down, against my hip. Kroth remained blasé upon the crinkling, covered chair across from me.

"Oh, I've read your little book, Solomon. You think there's a fucking cult in town that worships, what, *pollution*?"

"You already know the truth, detective. It was, as they say, an inside job headed by members of your own second district police department. It began after Flight 389 went down and Snavely shared his ancient, miserable wisdom with this city. Those first responders saw something, detective. Their eyes—haven't you ever noticed how odd, how incurious, they look? And what about what your friend, Guidry? Well, every kingdom needs its fool. The Dunnstown population at large knows nothing about what goes on in Treasure Forest, of course, until they start dying off, suffocated by the paper mill days. Then the good folks in your police department pay them a little visit, and take them on a trip to Treasure Forest. Tell me, how many truly elderly people have you seen in town, detective?"

"Not many," I replied. "Expect they either stay inside, they move or the air kills them."

"Partially correct, detective. Many of the suffering, non-killed elderly and young do indeed remain indoors, convalescing with oxygen tanks like mine. Many unable to take more than three steps before needing respiratory aid. The Brotherhood takes these non-killed to Treasure Forest once they exhibit all the signs. These paper mill days are getting worse and longer every year, as that which inhabits the air we breathe grows more palpable, more potent. And the non-killed population of Dunnstown gets sicker. Like me. Like me."

"Quite a conspiracy theory. The corpses. This... you're expecting me to believe that the second district PD skeletonized them?"

"Not the Brotherhood but that which they... well, worship isn't the right word for it. You see, your organization—the cult, if you will—believes in this pollution peculiar to Dunnstown as the ultimate manifestation of the Eternal. Connecting everything together. A hollow tree that has nothing to do with the living but everything to do with growth."

"But then what do the skeletons do to...?"

"To the suffering non-killed—the elderly and the young who fall early victim to the paper mill days? Do you know anything about infusoria, detective—the tiny organisms that are cultivated to feed fish fry? A biological process creates them—a little rot here, a little bacteria there. A similar process is occurring in Dunnstown. Human infusoria—these altered, appendaged skeletons—produce the vapor or smoke or fog effect we see, especially in Treasure Forest. Ultimately, all the skeletons are rendered hollow shells, which break apart. These pieces of ash in the air," and here he produced the test tube from earlier. "These are the remains of the transmuted dead. The tainted air feeds the infusoria, transforming vulnerable Dunnstowners into living skeletons. But the fog itself, it has so many names: the Origami, Daddy Longlegs, Snavely's Ultimate Ventriloquist. It turns the skeletons into more of itself. That's the punchline. It's exponential. Every year more of the non-killed transition, every year blacker fog, and one day *all* the residents will change. And when that final transformation comes, the whole town—everything in it and below it—will awaken from this borrowed reality into another one."

I'd heard enough. I finally raised my firearm.

"Okay, Kroth. Put your hands on top of your head, stand up slowly, and get down on the floor. On your belly."

Kroth didn't move. "You want to know the extent of what the Black Fog can do, detective? I'm no Greater Ventriloquist, but I've learned a few things from Joseph Snavely's book. Let me show you."

"Shut up and get your ass on the floor!" I yelled. "Hands on the top of your head, motherfucker! Now!"

But Kroth remained impassive, sitting with his legs crossed upon the high-back, Victorian-style chair.

"I think not, detective. Ha. But *you're* always thinking, aren't you, Raphaella? Mulling over the abuse you endured as a child, your misanthropic nature, the notable instances of brutality you committed both before and after you took up your occupation. Oh, I've done quite a bit of research on you over the past two days. I know all about those offenses, all about your so-called life to date. Your generally unsocial behavior. The ten instances of insubordination throughout your law enforcement career. Your rather laudable lack of interest in spawning a child and spewing it out into this dung heap of a world. The fact that your one and only friend in the world is also the man you very well may murder tomorrow. Clear that away, detective. It is nothing. Static. Now, close your eyes."

"The fuck are you doing to me? Stop or I'll..."

"Shoot? No, not yet you won't. You're closing your eyes now, little dummy. There. Now continue to listen to the sound of my voice as you relax your arms. *Don't bury me.* You know what to do next, don't you? Bend those elbows and stick the barrel of that now upside down firearm right there against the bridge of your own nose. That's it. *Don't bury me.* You can feel the wide, cool mouth of the pistol forming a perfect O—the perfect O of nothingness you will soon realize you always were. *Don't buh-bury me.* All this nonsense, the nonsense of a life badly lived, comes to an end, little dummy. Now. *Burn me*. Pull that trigger."

And—eyes clenched closed as instructed—I did pull it. There was a gun report, much quieter than I ever had imagined it would be. But then I opened my eyes and witnessed the extent of the fucking magic trick the old librarian had pulled off.

Because my arms had remained extended in front of me after all, pointing at a Victorian-style, high back chair, its once clear sheeting now colored with a spray of blood and brain matter. Kroth's body lay sprawled on the crinkly, plastic covered carpet. One side of his face was meat and his remaining eye stared up at nothing, his mouth ajar.

Then I started to hear something other than the ringing in my ears. Ever been in a car with a failing AC compressor? There's a kind of high-pitched whine that slowly turns into a distorted shriek. A sound no kind of animal, human or otherwise, could make. That's the closest I can come to what I was hearing in Kroth's living room.

The blood pulsating out of the librarian's body was odd looking, too thick, and it was far too dark. I began to cough, unable to quite catch my breath. The air, like Kroth's blood, had thickened imperceptibly at first, especially around his corpse, which was expelling dark snow. And now Kroth's corpse began convulsing and screeching, shedding and splitting its skin in violent convulsions. Growing... *longer.*

At first I couldn't get the fucking skull to stop screaming no matter what I did. Then I realized what I needed to do.

Burn me, Kroth had said.

I started tearing down the heavy plastic sheeting from the walls, the furniture the floor, wrapping the flopping corpse in it until the thing could barely move. The screaming had become impossibly loud, and I was sure my ears would soon be bleeding from it. Something black and jagged was starting to cut through all those layers of sheeting. I dragged the bucking, growing skeleton-thing through the dining room to the den's fireplace. And that's where I thrust it, right up the chimney. Now the shrieking wasn't quite as loud but echoed in a way that made me want to vomit and shit myself simultaneously.

My hands shaking, I struggled to light the fireplace's long electric lighter, clicking it over and over to no avail.

Those convulsive, growing limbs were tearing the body free of the plastic sheeting. I pulled out my Glock and emptied the clip into the thing. That slowed its movement down but didn't do much to quell the shrieking or my panic.

Now I was back to trying to light the goddamn fire. And then it hit me. Not enough oxygen in the house.

Oxygen. I found four green, mottled tanks tucked in a kitchen nook beside the oven. I pulled the hoses out of three of the tanks, turned the valves up and stuck a couple of them up the chimney with the jerking skeleton-thing. Black, bony appendages like too skinny, too sharp finger bones were ripping through the sheeting as the unholy shriek rose in volume. Cracks were appearing in the bricks of the fireplace. I rolled another hissing tank towards the jerking body and took the other one for myself.

At a safe distance, I finally lit the lighter and approached the fireplace. The little flame grew longer and longer the further into the oxygen-infused den I got. I grabbed a newspaper from a stack of them, lit it and tossed it at the fireplace.

I didn't wait to see if my aim was true but hauled ass out the front door and towards the cruiser. Coughing like hell, I jumped in, turned the engine over (three times before it would start) and floored it. About a minute later I heard and felt the detonation.

You didn't know that was my doing, did you? I heard something about a neighborhood gas line explosion on the cop radio the next day, but I cut it off before I got details. You bet I feel like shit about it, but what the fuck would you have done in my place?

I woke up in my kitchen wrapped around the spare oxygen tank, its dial indicating that I had huffed from it liberally before I passed out. Don't remember much about getting back home at all.

I do remember the dream I had though. Tiny, black skeletons floating in the dirty water of a small, red aquarium. Me looking at them through one of the circular, built-in magnifying glasses. As the tiny bodies grew larger to my eye, I realized that they were replicas of the Treasure Forest skeletons. Jet black corpses, appendaged— growing longer, their extremities taking on strange, new forms as I watched. Then the water in the tank became a kind of semitransparent fog, then soil, and I was in Treasure Forest again. No old paper mill or trees or vegetation of any kind were visible. All that remained were skeletal faces just above the brown, toxic soil, as far as I could see, blowing black air and ashes out of their open mouths and hollow eyes. And I could hear and feel their squirming skeletons growing beneath me.

- 6 -

When I awoke, the paper mill days were over. It had rained while I had slept. The ground was wet, the sky was clear, the air dry and cool and fresh. But I felt the paper mill days lingering beneath my skin, within my bones.

I headed out with Kroth's oxygen tank in my backseat. Didn't bother much with the radio, again full of activity after another deadly paper mill day.

I went straight to the empty police station. Took a military-grade gas mask, a protective suit and gloves from Forensics without checking them out (had to pound off a couple of locks—no one there to stop me). Grabbed a chainsaw, ten gallons of gasoline and drove out to Treasure Forest. I huffed oxygen and albuterol for a couple of minutes, donned my mask and other protective gear, and hiked up the steep hill. The ground was still covered in smoke up there, and the flakes were suspended in the air around the mill in spite of the clear sky beyond it.

My Glock was in hand with extra clips to spare.

Entering the structure felt like falling into the depths of outer space. I had thought of everything but lighting. When I turned around to go back to the cruiser, though, I saw something glowing near the base of the old digester. It appeared to be a flashlight lying maybe twenty feet in front of me, like a comet in the void—black, ash-like dust motes floating like tiny corpses in its trail.

I was walking towards that beam a long time. Then the light failed and went out. I heard a hollow click and a slow, grating wheeze, followed by Guidry's voice, bubbling as if underwater.

"So... So sorry, Raph," Guidry said. He sounded like he was about to cry—or giggle. "The boys, they told me only the old folks would need to be changed. But I guess now it's going to be everyone."

I cocked my gun.

"The skeletons—the bodies we found around Treasure Forest? They were prepared—*prepared*. By the 2nd District and... and something in this mill or maybe... maybe below it. It makes em ready. But they're not alive afterwards. They're *real*. Oh, Raphie, This factory—it's adding something to Treasure Forest and—

something is adding it to the air. The whole town. Never knew much about it myself, but I figure the boys don't really know either. But I'm kind of gettin' it now, Raphie. By becoming one with dead stuff—the Fog, it wants us to become... like it. Something *real*. Can you hear its voice, Raphie? There it is. I can hear the Black Fog."

Guidry fell silent, and I had arrived maybe five feet (or five light years) from him. Then my foot came in contact with his flashlight in the dark. I picked it up and pounded it with the butt of my gun, and it sputtered to life. I pointed the beam towards where I had heard Guidry's voice. But the thing on the littered pulp mill floor was not my partner.

The diminutive skeleton—head half broken open, exposing a pulley and some kind of wooden mechanism within—sprawled on the ground, staring into the flashlight's beam. Segmented limbs were folded into themselves like a dead spider's.

Snap. The open mouth shut and opened again. And it spoke with the voice of my partner, bubbling, thin and reedy. Its black eyes were rolling.

"Don't... Don't let it put me together."

Then I heard a familiar shriek rising in the darkness along with a heavy flailing crash across the void. I flipped the flashlight towards the sounds and watched as the fat body of my partner, Michael Thomas Guidry, pushed itself into a corroded paper machine. Already bloody and growing bloodier, it thrashed against splintered beams and corroded pipes. Guidry's body was transforming—limbs elongating to twice their length, black digits clawing out of misshapen hands and twisting feet. Skin peeling off. Guidry's distorted face with the rolling, impossible button eyes of an idiot doll or a shark.

I put six bullets into my partner's body—into what my partner's body was becoming. Yet the thing continued shrieking. I shot again—first to the neck, then three times to the torso. It fell to the floor, twitching, but it still screamed. And it was still growing.

Meanwhile, the shattered, child-dummy-spider-thing's mouth was clicking. Open, closed. Open, closed. I marched it to the mill's great digester, dumped it in and emptied out my gas cans in there as well. Lit the digester up and the dummy with it.

Then I began working on Guidry's body.

Though the thing could do no more than jerk every now and then, as its bones grew longer and weirder, the skull was still shrieking like a failing air compressor. But I had planned for that. Industrial strength earplugs. They almost made the sound bearable as I cut Guidry's body to pieces with my chainsaw in the digester's firelight.

Can't remember much more. I was sobbing. Pipes were hissing, sputtering dark fluid above me. A great squealing static roared in the darkness around me. Or maybe it was just the sound of my chainsaw cutting.

When I came to myself again, I was still separating appendages—some fingers, some toes, some claws and some less defined things—from hands, hands from forearms and sub-forearms from segmented insect legs and deformed claws... tossing them all to the mill fire. And then I dumped that shrieking skull itself into the digester's inferno.

At some point I was incapacitated by a few of my fellow police, members of the Brotherhood who came a little late to the party but soon enough to stop me from completing my good work. I never had time to finish annihilating all the squirming bones of my partner. I never had a chance to burn the factory to the ground.

Afterwards, as I'm sure you know, I confessed to the murder of my partner. You can add Kroth and whoever else might've died in his neighborhood's gas line explosion to the list now.

I took their psychiatric tests, and they told me I was competent to stand trial. Officially, I knew what I was doing when I shot Guidry's body and started dissecting and immolating it. And I did know what I was doing.

There was some deception on my part, I admit, through silence if nothing else. I never denied the bullshit story that Guidry and I were involved in a long term affair and that he had finally broken it off. Made them think I was taking psychotic revenge on him by saying I wanted to erase his body from the earth, but that part was true. They also suggested I was to blame for abducting and murdering the other skeletonized victims and for distorting their bodies in the most grotesque ways. There wasn't any believable proof, of course. But I never denied any of it.

You know the rest of the story as it played out in front of the media. Scorned sociopathic lady cop offs her partner-lover. Just like Kroth said at the end—all those things I obsessed over for so long finally came to light. The abuse I endured as a child, "my unsociable nature, a notable instance of brutality," blah blah blah. And, of course, the simple fact of being a lady policeman killer. A *scorned* lady policeman killer to boot.

But now you've come to interview me here in the clink, and I'm curious. First, I assumed you wanted to know why I really killed Guidry. Then I figured maybe you wanted to hear about the skeletons. Maybe you had found out what they're like—how they shriek and thrash around and *grow*. I assumed you wanted to know about the toxic garbage that poured out of those corpses and maybe about the Brotherhood of the Black Fog itself. Most of all, I was hoping you'd whisk me to some federal lockup far away from foggy, farty Dunnstown.

But I can tell by that blank expression—by those eyes of a doll and a fucking shark—that you already know everything you need to know.

Organ Void

"What is missing at this moment?"

Rose snorts as she drives her Bug home from work. The gentle voice of a self-help guru drones over her car speakers.

"What is missing at this moment?"

The question buzzes through her consciousness as Rose navigates down the sooty Interstate exit. Beyond that—the whining roar of the mammoth overpasses loom above her like ruined cathedrals.

"What is missing at this moment?"

"ORGAN -VOID"

Both words are emphatic. Underlined in deep black, the letters slanted to the right on the wrinkled face of the cardboard.

(*"...there is nothing else, and at that moment when you fully realize..."*)

The fingers that hold the sign are long but look as wide as Rose's big toes, the lengthy nails oddly well-manicured. The man or woman (it's impossible to tell which) holding the sign has a ragged face browned from years of unprotected sun exposure. The eyes entirely covered by a tumorous mass of wrinkles, giving the impression of visionary blindness. (*"...dead to the aliveness in others. And so we can no longer have..."*) The mouth a tight line in a face that retains a fine—almost aristocratic—bone structure, ample chin, broad, high cheekbones and square jaw framed by wild, chest-long, dingy hair spilling in every direction.

Man or woman, Rose thinks, You were beautiful once.

The tramp is one of the skinniest human beings Rose has ever seen in spite of hands and a face that retain the illusion of weight. (*"...pain body has two ways of feeding..."*) Only hard junk use coupled with starvation could achieve such a skeletal frame. The clothes the vagrant wears—dingy gray, hole-ridden wife-beater, stained cargo shorts and flip-flops—only highlight the form's emaciation.

"*ORGAN -VOID*"

What does it mean? A medical condition? An expression of loss?

Rose rolls down the window, expecting the traditional whiff of urine, excrement and/or strong alcohol. ("*...ultimate thing is the realization of the formless essence...*") But only the pungent smell of vehicle exhaust meets her. The vagrant shuffles towards the Bug—those thick, manicured fingers still grasping the cardboard sign on either side, pushing it through the open window.

"Uh, hi there," says Rose, pulling her face back from the cardboard just inches away. "I'd like to buy your sign for... will twenty dollars do it?" This has long been Rose's practice, thus simultaneously appeasing her distaste at giving the homeless something for nothing and her guilt at not helping them in any way. She has boxes full of such signs—but never one like this.

There's no response from the tramp, who continues holding the sign uncomfortably close to Rose's face. ("*...the mind made image 'little me'...*") The cardboard smells moist, like rubbing alcohol masking pus.

"*ORGAN -VOID*"

The traffic light turns green, and immediate, fierce honking commences behind Rose's old VW.

"Oh damn," Rose says, her hands shaking as she digs deep into her purse for bills. "I've got, um, forty. Will forty do?"

"Come on, goddamnit! Move - your - ass!" ("*...useless when we talk about this. That's why...*") A chorus of beeping and engine gunning echoes across the cyclopean overpass-wasteland, the single eyes of the daddy longlegs street lights glaring down.

Sagging cardboard falls into Rose's lap, and she cringes. Pushes her proffered bills toward the bum. But the figure withdraws with surprising speed—long, skeletal arms and large, thick hands hanging limp now, head tilted back, mouth agape in an attitude of surrender—a junk-ravaged scarecrow at the end of the Interstate ramp. ("*...that deepest Self, not the mind made self. It's so precious...*")

The light turns red while Rose stares at the vagrant, and the drivers behind her scream and honk and rumble in vehicular berserker rage. A man exits the truck behind her—a short, stocky shark of a brute. Rose balls up the two twenties and throws them towards the sign-bearer. She doesn't wait to see if they find their mark or are blown away by the hot highway winds. ("...*the 'voice in my head' is not who I am. Who am I then?"*) Rose guns her puttering car to life, punches the power button on her stereo to silence the droning self-help guru and runs the light, almost broadsiding a fast-moving motorcycle. She races home the rest of the way to outpace the wrathful drivers in the wake of her Bug.

She is taking in huge gulps of air all the way home. Adrenaline like too potent junk jacking her heart rate. Rose doesn't look down at the bum's sign until she parks on the street in front of her ramshackle, duplex apartment.

"ORGAN -VOID"

"My name is Dr. Onavi. You've had an episode."

A roaring vibration grows and subsides. A chill. The smell of dirt or dust that makes her nose twitch. A floating sensation and the slow awareness of her body on an unyielding, rough surface. Rose feels a kind of wonder. No running commentary peels off rapid-fire auctioneer-style in her head. There are no words that come to mind. There are no words.

"Gord Onavi."

Rose opens her eyes, sees the dark shapes above her. All concrete and metal framed in the bright LED and sodium lights of the city, grooved, mammoth steel, concrete crossbeams. It is cold. The crossbeams bleed dark mold. With effort, Rose rises to a sitting position, and looks around her. She peers up at the underbelly of the Interstate, each track of road at various levels in a pattern that seems altogether random, senseless. She notices her bare legs for the first time, grimy, scratched up and thin. Rose braces herself for support to keep from collapsing back to the littered concrete as it reels around her. She is wearing only her long t-shirt (the blue "Captain Hook's Seafood" tee with the eye-patched pirate head emblazoned in white). Her underwear is gone.

"Can you hear me, Rose?"

How did she get here? Downtown by the looks of it, just off

Poydras Street in the long strip of city properties. Makeshift parking lots, impoundment yards, RV parks. And the homeless, of course. Blocks and blocks of them, spread out. One woman at the Interstate onramp on one knee, eyes closed and head held up to the smog-sick sky. Filthy, gloved hands crossed and twitching. Bowlegged and hooded figures with overflowing bags full of mysterious odds and ends.

"You may call me Dr. Gord. Am I reaching you, Rose?"

Rose rises to her bare feet, walking on the cold, sometimes muddy concrete, puddles shining in the sodium glare. The roadway above her is quiet—only the intermittent sound of vehicle dopplering. The drainage pipes under the Interstate shattered from some nameless deluge. The cityscape breathes.

"You may experience some pain now, Rose, or feel some pressure."

Cold. Barren. Desolate. Rose hears and feels the repetition of the words like a mantra inside her otherwise quiet mind. If she feels pain or pressure it is only from her hungry guts, her scraped and battered legs and the aching pain in the side of her neck. Cold. Barren. Desolate. These words don't touch the quiescence within her. She staggers on as if purposeful, absorbed in every throb of discomfort and every nerve-thrill within her extremities. And there is a shape ahead—a tall and hunched human shape.

"A dithered wino youth vow?" the husky voice asks her.

"Are you down with the void?"

"Can you hear me, Rose?"

Rose wakes up late, alarm clock insect droning. Echoes of a recurring nightmare—something about titanic steel and concrete curtains above her. Her throat is raw with stinging phlegm. Did she piss herself in the night? Rose checks the dingy black futon sheets but finds no sign of moisture. She farts and sniffs—and smells something like rubbing alcohol and pus. It clings to the flesh-colored bedroom and stained, gray-salted wall to wall.

What is missing?

She calls in sick to work, her voice satisfactorily croaking on her boss's voicemail. Rose's stomach produces internal shitting and dribbling sounds... *oozing or spitting out of the mouths that appear on the organs in response to that awful pressure...* Her head hurts, a deep bone pain, throbbing as if in concert with the gastric ensemble within her abdomen. She totters into a shabby bathroom, hunched and holding her stomach as if gutshot. Squats on the toilet and immediately has waterrhea, which she examines for signs of blood, black bile or other damning viscera. Nothing—just the typical, medium flecks floating in light brown liquid. No sharp diarrhea stench, though, which Rose thinks odd. And she remembers the run-in with the street bum yesterday and that sign of his.

"*ORGAN -VOID*"

...organ almost certainly meaning vital organs either literally or figuratively that's the crux of the matter yes but either way in any event something is missing or else filled with empty space yes void or perhaps it means an end of sorts or a denial or correction...

An image from her nightmare comes to mind and more liquid hits the already hot toilet water and splashes back on her ass and upper thighs. Something about an overpass, a pock-marked gray series of rectangles and crossbeams curving down at the ends of her sight and contracting and expanding as if the lungs of some vile behemoth, the large, broken pipes carrying sewer water leaking black liquid like shit or jizz out of the cracks that appear from the shifting metal and cement.

...like writing VOID on a check that has been incorrectly filled out and then of course there's the implication of darkness yes the void of space and emptiness and all that comes of that but isn't there also the possibility of voiding like evacuation yes pissing or shitting and if an internal organ did that it would be squeezed out imagine like a sponge-kidney or dirt-liver grabbed and clenched and twisted like an old wet snot or cum rag the pus or bile oozing or splitting out of the mouths that appear on the organs in response to that fantastic pressure...

"Organ Void," Rose says aloud, shivering and groaning with nausea, coughing up greenish-yellow discharge. Yes, she's ill and likely with a fever to boot. She flushes the toilet again but there is no sucking spiral of liquid. Too much toilet paper and shit. Rose groans again, gambles on one last flush and squeals as the light brown liquid tops then overtops the toilet's rim.

...and where would all that organ piss that organ shit go why in the rest of the body always in the body and if all your organs start convulsively squeezing spitting out their vital juices into the rest of the organism what would that do

what would that feel like painful no doubt but after empty meaningless as in having no force all the life escaping from one container into a larger container...

The sharp gas pains come in waves, leaving a gap of about thirty seconds between them (Rose counts). In the interludes she is able to move, bare feet shit-tracking the bedroom then living room floors with steadily lighter shit-prints as she makes her way to the kitchen. She strains and fumbles for the medicine cupboard. Bottles of antidepressants and tranquilizers, vitamins and pain pills rattle and spill like slot machine coins onto the kitchen floor. She dry-pops three Imodiums and a couple of Vicodins, and the next gut-wave hits.

...never meant for the life-spillage that oozes or drips or rushes out of the organs the organs have voided themselves have created a void for themselves have made their existence invalid useless uninhabitable and imagine if such a creature such a life form kept on existing spreading their disease of unmentionable unnatural compression moving on like a balloon like a baboon bobbing along...

Rose slips on diarrhea and falls hard on the linoleum onto her hip, but she doesn't feel it. Her naked ass dribbles shit as she crawls through the carpeted living room, trying to beat the next gut-punch. Rose makes it to her bedroom and pops open her box, one of her boxes of signs. She can't even smell the old mildew or pungent cologne or vomit or piss—not even rubbing alcohol and pus. She pulls out the sign she's looking for, the one that's pushing and pushing her frenzied, sick mind. The gastric walloping begins again as she grabs the thing in both hands, clutches it close and fills her vision with those words:

"*ORGAN -VOID*"

...organ sap stored in extremities fermenting bile-wine beyond feeling maybe but maybe not maybe just thoughts the brain a large organ itself thought-nectar internally bleeding emptying the head but filling the body with mind nonsense that might feel like sewage blending with other sewage filling up the whorls and the body like a toilet overflowing the rim with sepsis-diarrhea like a body vomiting not outside but inside of itself...

"Am I reaching you?"

Rose awakens by degrees. She hears a steady roar of traffic above. She sweats. Hears groans and unintelligible muttering nearby.

She opens her eyes and sees an interstate overpass above, mid-morning. People, prone on thin, foam mattresses, dot the concrete pavement around her. The bodies—some with slim pillows under their heads, some not—are of varying ages. An elderly, bearded black man lies nearest to her, back arched as if in pain but unconscious, mouth agape, fixed in position. He wears the typical patient's wardrobe—a thin, dingy blue, diamond-patterned robe. A bored looking, middle-aged nurse in scrubs, hand on one hip, fans him with a piece of cardboard. On the other side of Rose a bald woman lies, shirtless and legless, upon her chest and face and outstretched arms. She appears to be in a posture of worship.

A small, bespectacled man with white, wiry hair, a round face and a prodigious belly ambles from one patient to another. His long white coat shines in the makeshift hospital. As Rose looks towards the physician, he returns her gaze. He smiles and his eyes crinkle shut.

"I'm glad to see you conscious, Rose. Onavi. Dr. Gord Onavi, but you may call me Dr. Gord."

"What... what happened, doctor?" Rose asks.

"You've had an episode, Rose," the doctor replies, squatting down to check her pulse, and his hands feel cool and dry. "Forgive the mobile unit. Cuts cuts cuts coming down. Though paradoxically this is where we're supposed to be, yes—with the street people, the suffering non-killed who can't or won't come to us."

"An episode? What kind of episode?"

"A reaction."

"To a drug?"

"Indeed."

"But I don't remember taking anything."

"In your case, that makes perfect sense."

"I don't understand. What happened, doctor?"

"*Organ Void*," Dr. Onavi whispers.

"Wait, that... that was a sign."

"Oh yes, quite a bit of fluid entered your extremities last night. You certainly have all the signs."

"No, it was *a* sign, like from a homeless person. 'Organ Void.'"

"That's exactly how it's contracted, my dear. But—"

"I thought you said it was a drug. Wait. How are you treating me?"

"I'm not here to treat you. I am only observing. After all, we can't avoid the unavoidable, now can we?"

The bald, legless woman turns her face towards Rose and smiles toothlessly. She asks, "Is she down with the void?"

"Indeed she is, Mrs. Smoot," the doctor replies, eyes crinkling, patting Rose's shoulder. "But not to worry. Her ill-directed mind is being righted by degrees."

Rose listens to the traffic above. A deep peace moves within her.

"An ill-directed mind."

The self-help guru's voice is droning on through Rose's Bug.

"An ill-directed mind."

Rose navigates the sooty Interstate exit, and—beyond that—the whining roar of the mammoth overpasses looming above her like ruined cathedrals. The one-eyed, daddy longlegs streetlights observe her as they make their ambling way back and forth along the overpasses down ramps and back again.

"An ill-directed mind."

Rose grips the peeling steering wheel, and it grips her back with segmented, white-painted legs. The leg-hooks in her fingers impart a sense of solidity. Her hands feel full and substantial on the wheel. Both her expansive, bare feet are melded into the segmented pedals below. Rose does not shift gears as she navigates the great, sweeping Interstate-ramp-bridges that curve down and up, left and right in soothing waves. Few vehicles but hers can be seen or heard on the roadways. Rose observes without thought, without judgment, that her car stereo is missing, now only a black rectangle in the sloping dashboard.

"An ill-directed mind."

A solitary homeless man—grizzled, hooded and junk-sick—stands at the blinking traffic light. Rose pulls one hand free, steering wheel legs popping with an un-zippering sound. Tiny hooks or insect appendages fall twitching from the tops of her broad fingers down to the thick, black shag of the floorboard. Rose's Bug slows down as she opens her glove compartment—humid and warm inside—and draws out her sign. The driver's side window rolls down automatically as she pulls to a stop. The man, handlebar mustache drooping, gazes wide-eyed upon Rose, but extends a quaking palm nonetheless.

"An ill-directed mind," Rose says.

"Sorry, ma'am? Can you, uh, can you spare anything?"

"*Organ Void*," Rose says.

The homeless man drops his hand. "I ain't down with the void. No ma'am."

"*Organ Void*," Rose says again, and gives him her sign.

The man's bloodshot eyes water as his trembling hands take the flimsy, corrugated cardboard. It stinks of rubbing alcohol and pus. Rose pulls away, and the man, now slumped over, weeping, raises the sign to chest level. New insect legs push out from the peeling steering wheel and inject their hooked ends into Rose's broad fingers.

Rose will keep driving up and down and below the Interstate, looking for the junk-sick, the despairing, the ill-directed, the suffering non-killed. Rose will show them the new way to be.

"What is missing at this moment?"

The spoken question comes unbidden from no source Rose can name, but the answer comes to her mind—from beyond it—almost immediately:

"Nothing. Nothing is missing at this moment."

Nothing at all.

The Secret of Ventriloquism

A Play in 1 Act

CHARACTERS

JOSEPH SNAVELY	A lesser ventriloquist
REGGIE McRASCAL	Joe's ventriloquist dummy
MARGARET	Joe's lady-friend
MR. VOX	A Greater Ventriloquist

SCENES

Joseph's bedroom	Scene 1	Early evening
The Night Airport	Scene 2	One hour later
Joseph's bedroom	Scene 3	Early evening
Joseph's bedroom	Scene 4	Midnight
The Factory	Scene 5	Evening
The Factory (and a Dream)	Scene 6	Some weeks later

SCENE 1

(A cottage bedroom, early evening. Joe is sitting on a stool, facing the audience, in front of a large, see-through mirror frame that hangs center stage. Reggie is perched on Joe's knee. The ventriloquist dummy is wearing a Halloween costume with diaphanous wings, bat ears and sparkles.)

JOE
(Clears throat.)
Good evening ladies and gentlemen, boys and girls, and welcome!

REG
Introducing Joseph Snavely, whose "20 Simple Steps to Vinkelikism" will go into your head and into your heart. And they won't do your stomach any good either.

JOE
(annoyed)
And this is my ventriloquist doll, Reggie McRascal.

REG
Doll? Can you do *this*?
			(turns his head all the way around)

JOE
What? Of course not!

REG
That's funny.

JOE
What's so funny about that?

REG

I thought all dummies could.

JOE

Quiet. Now let's get on with today's lesson, young man. Do you remember which step we were on?

REG

Sorry, Jo-Jo. I just can't do any practice step thingies today.

JOE

Why not?

REG

Because today I'm in love.

JOE

You're in love? You mean...

REG
(bending close to JOE's face as if closely examining something)
What's that on your nose?

JOE
(nervously)
It's a freckle.

REG

It's crawling.

JOE
(slapping his nose, annoyed)
It's not crawling.

REG

I'm not kidding about being in love.

JOE
(fondly)
Love.

REG
Yeah, y'know there's nothing like turning the lights down
low.

JOE
I know.

REG
Smooching a little.

JOE
Smooching?

REG
Sure, then you sit in the loving room...

JOE
Loving room? That's *living.*

REG
You said it! That's *living!*

JOE
Never mind! Tell me something...
(REG bends close to JOE's face again)
I...

REG
Your freckle has a friend now.

JOE
Now stop that, Reg! Tell me about your girl.

REG

Whaddaya wanna know?

JOE

Just some simple little thing.

REG

That's her! That's my girl!

JOE

No, I mean some peculiar characteristic.

REG

Well, she bites her nails.

JOE

A lot of girls bite their nails.

REG

Toenails?

JOE

Is that the silliest thing you're going to say tonight?

REG

Nope, but it's the funniest. That's right, if you haven't laughed yet, that's the act, ladies and gentlemen. Well, good night.
(starts to leave)

JOE
(holding onto Reg)

Wait a minute.

REG

Get your goddamn hands off my shirt.

JOE

Reggie! Language!

REG

Yeah yeah yeah. Speaking of foul language, what about *your* girl, Joey? What's her name?

JOE

Margaret. And she's *not* my girl—she's my *lady* friend.

REG

Lady? Ha! She's no lady. And you complain about *my* potty mouth.

JOE

Show a little respect, Reggie. You know, I think it's high time we get on with today's lesson and speak a few words about Mr. Vox.

REG

Oh, yeah! Mr. Box! That guy really freaks me out!

JOE

Not Box - *Vox*. And that's exactly who we've got to talk to these good folks about, right?

REG

Is this one of them steps to vin... vinkelteltism?

JOE

Ventriloquism.

REG

That's what I said. Hey, what's that in the mirror?
(squinting)

JOE

Is this another one of your jokes?

REG

Naw, naw. Just something I see when I stare real real hard without closing my eyes — like, uh, I dunno... some kind of black fog or somethin'.

JOE

(alarmed)

No no, Reggie. Blink, blink. If you ever see black fog in a mirror, you'll want to look away. Just ignore it. That's right. And that goes for you good folks too.

REG

(blinking and trying not to look at the mirror)

Alright alright. Is this one of them steps to vinkelteltism?

JOE

The word is *Ventriloquism*. And no, it's not, or maybe it's a secret step.

(Turning back to audience)

You see, my aspiring ventriloquism apprentices, you need help. You may understand that mastery of ventriloquism takes many thousands of days of continuous practice, but—trust me on this—your family and friends *won't* understand, not even your current or potential lady friend.

REG

Ha! You can say that again! Why you shoulda heard Joe's gal, ARGH-aret.

JOE

Margaret. Now would you please just quiet down and listen?

REG

Alright alright! Jesus Christ.

JOE

Reggie! Language!

REG

Yeah yeah yeah...

JOE

That's better.

> (clearing his throat, addressing audience through mirror)

You've got to find yourself a *real* mentor, friends. Someone who can guide you through the difficult steps ahead. A Master Ventriloquist. Bear with me. An open mind is key to your future mastery of Greater Ventriloquism.

REG

A hole in the head don't hurt neither.

JOE

> (trying to ignore REG)

You see, after years of fruitless research and disappointment, I found my own mentor one memorable night in the unlikeliest of ways. As with any other late evening, I was sleeping in the bed next to my lady friend, Margaret...

> (REG is pulled off stage right, as if floating, and JOE stands up from the stool, which is pulled off stage left, also as if floating. The bed behind JOE flips onto its bottom end, giving the audience a bird's eye view of it. A stuffed dog rests at JOE's feet. JOE, still standing, leans back next to a sleeping MARGARET and pulls the covers over himself, still addressing the audience.)

...our pet dog resting against my feet just as I trained it to do—and I was dreaming.

SCENE 2

(The bed, with MARGARET and JOE's dog still in it, is pulled up above and out of sight, leaving JOE standing. The bedroom set and JOE's ventriloquist suit split in half simultaneously. The revealed set suggests a mid-size airport late at night. JOE is now wearing a black tuxedo and inserts a large earpiece into one ear. The shadows of passengers come and go behind and around JOE.)

JOE

Passengers were disappearing from the airport—especially people arriving and departing on late night flights. These disappearances were linked to a terrible catastrophe that was inevitable if my mission failed. And as I conducted my investigation, I became aware that the passengers and the flight attendants, the pilots, the security guards and ticket tellers and even the airport itself *did not seem real.*

REG
(voice over)
Hello! Of course not! It was a *dream*!

JOE
(addressing REG, offstage)
No no no, Reg. *I was in no way aware that I was dreaming* but was convinced that the airport and all the people in it *were not real.* I felt an otherworldly *wrongness* in everything.

REG
(voice over, chuckling)

JOE
(ignoring REG, to audience again)
My employer, via secret agent earpiece, informed me that

the secret of the night-airport disappearances was reportedly buried somewhere on the grounds between the short term parking decks and the departing floor of the airport terminal. This suited me fine, as it meant I could continue to work in relative solitude, away from the unnerving airport un-persons.

> (JOE walks through automatic glass doors, suggesting that he is now outside. A strong wind blows in from offstage.)

As I walked through the automatic glass doors, a soundless helicopter with indistinct lettering upon it swooped over the parking deck and landed on one side of the otherwise empty arrival roadway.

> (MR. VOX, a large, tall man in a dark business suit and mirrored sunglasses strides towards JOE, holding out a huge, gloved, right hand as if offering assistance. JOE shies away.)

MR. VOX
(in a distant, echoing monotone.)
My name is Vox. Let me help you.

> (As MR. VOX—moving closer—reaches out, JOE thrusts his right arm out in an attempt to block MR. VOX's hidden left hand. JOE realizes too late that MR. VOX's extended right hand now holds a large syringe and needle, which MR. VOX plunges into the side of JOE's neck. Blackout.)

This will help me put you together.

> (Tight spotlight on JOE's head as he begins to twist his head back and forth. Stage whisper.)

None of this is happening.

SCENE 3

(Lights up. The bed, with MARGARET still in it, is lowered behind JOE, still on its end, facing the audience. The bedroom set closes in front of the airport set and JOE's tuxedo splits to reveal his ventriloquist outfit. JOE, still standing, covers himself up as if in bed.)

JOE

After the dream's conclusion—far from coming to my conscious senses—my feelings of unreality grew more distinct and acute with every waking moment.

MR. VOX
(voiceover)
My name is Vox. *This will help me put you together.*

JOE
(tight spot on Margaret's sleeping head.)
Margaret was in the throes of her own private dream, as I lay paralyzed next to her. Suddenly her movements stopped as the gaping, dark holes of her eyes locked onto mine.

MARGARET
(in MR. VOX's voice)
Nothing was talking as Vox. It was talking through him.

JOE
(REG—eyes closed as if asleep—invisibly enters, floating in from offstage right, nestling into JOE's arms.)
Since that night, there have been so many more nighttime experiences like this—so many lessons learned the hard way, and a great deal of exhausting pain and fear. But remember...

(picking up pen and paper and writing as he

talks)

"STEP 10: Don't be discouraged. Suffering and exhaustion are both key to your future mastery of Greater Ventriloquism."

(addressing audience again)

And pay attention to your *own* dreams, ladies and gentlemen. Your ventriloquist mentor will find you just like Mr. Vox found me. Just you wait and see.

SCENE 4

(JOE's and MARGARET's bedroom, late at
night. JOE is sitting in front of the
transparent mirror on the foot of the bed,
slumped over without a shirt on in old, torn,
red boxers. Reggie sits on Joe's knee, still in
his Halloween costume. Both figures appear
to be asleep. A stuffed dog lies at JOE's feet.
A door slams offstage left, waking both JOE
and REG with a start. Sound of dishes being
stuffed roughly into a sink. MARGARET,
wearing a pink business suit and heels, storms
into the room.)

MARGARET

Fuck!

REG

Language! Language!

MARGARET

You asshole. You could've at least loaded the goddamned
dishwasher.

REG

Language! Lan—!
(JOE covers REG's mouth with a sheepish
grin.)

MARGARET

How about you put that little fucker down for a second and
get some shit done around here?

JOE
(Calmly)
Margaret, you're upset...

MARGARET

You're goddamned right I'm upset, Joe! It's bad enough you waking me up in the middle of the night to tell me about your boring ass nightmares on and on, but the house looks like shit! I mean, what have you been doing all day?

JOE

Honey-pie, that's not really fair. You know I've been working on this skit for the Halloween show. It's taken a lot of diligent work to put it together.

MARGARET

Work? Work? *I* work twelve fucking hours a day—twelve fucking hours—in a soulless, corporate law firm no less, because *you* can't seem to hold down a real job. I mean, I'm working all the fucking time here, and you're sitting around the house playing with that creepy doll all day and night.

REG

Doll? Can you do *this*?
        (turns his head all the way around)

JOE

Darling, we've been through this over and over again. Reggie is a dummy, not a doll. And ventriloquism *is* indeed a real job. Not only that, it's a difficult job that takes hundreds and...

MARGARET

Oh yeah. I know, I know. Hundreds and *thousands* of hours, right?

JOE

Baby, that's...
        (Pouts)
Well, ok. You're totally right.

MARGARET

Don't do that baby shit. You *manipulate* me, Joseph, do you know that? This fucking passive aggressive, martyr bullshit. I know what you're doing.

REG

What?

MARGARET
(Without missing a beat)
You're changing the fucking subject just like you always do. You're trying to make me feel guilty when *you're* to blame, but—you know what? It's been three goddamn years now, Joe. Do you realize that? Three fucking years.

REG

Language! Language!
(A tense pause)

MARGARET

Joseph Robert Snavely, so help me god, if you don't stop correcting me like I'm a goddamned animal through that piece of shit doll of yours, I am going to pull its ugly fucking head off and throw it through the goddamned window. I *mean* it.

JOE
(Placing a protective right arm around Reggie's torso)
Fine, sweetie. I'm sorry. You know I'm not feeling well right now, and you know I'm not *sleeping* well. What I said about that airport last night, remember? It'll all be ok soon, though. Mr. Vox said... I mean... I'll get more ventriloquist gigs soon. It's just that...

MARGARET

More "gigs?" And how much money do you bring home from those? Next to nothing, that's how much. You're not even making sense half the time anymore, Joe. All this crazy shit about your dreams and this what's his name? Mr. Fox?

JOE
Vox.

MARGARET
Look, I think you need help, Joe. You're like a fucking toddler—not a man. I'm sorry, but you're just not pulling your weight around here, Joe, and you haven't for a long goddamned time.

REG
(Eyelids suggestively half open, bushy eyebrows moving up and down)
Aw, that's not true, toots! Joey's *fulltime* job is to make yer sexy tush happy, if you know what I mean! Rowr. Rowr.

(Pause.)

MARGARET
(addressing REG)
Joey's fulltime job is to make my 'sexy tush happy'? Well, ya know what, Reg old buddy old pal? Joey hasn't been doing *that* job right for quite some time now either. If you know what I mean.
(REG bursts into gales of hysterical laughter as JOE stares agape, speechless.)
I can't do this anymore, Joe. I'm sorry. You'd better leave.

REG
(screeching)
WHO IS HE?

MARGARET
(shocked)
What? Who's who?

REG
The guy you're... *fucking.*

(Margaret is speechless. And guilty.)

JOE
(Formally)
Well, well. Now I understand.
>(JOE pulls a battered fake-leather trunk from under the bed and carefully places REG and a few pieces of clothing inside it. He turns to MARGARET.)

Be seeing you... *Animal-dummy.*
>(MARGARET and the bedroom set are pulled off, leaving an empty scrim behind JOE, holding his trunk. JOE addresses the transparent mirror in front of him.)

And that, as they say, is that. I had been so confident—so cocksure—that I knew how to work my lady friend inside and out like the dummy she was (and is).

REG
(from inside the trunk)
"Confidence" and "cock" ain't never been your forte, Jo-Jo!

JOE
(pulling REG out of the trunk)
Very funny. But as you may recall I did have complete control over Margaret at one time.

REG
Ha! But not as much as you thought you did, eh schmucko?

JOE

I probably just lost interest.

REG

Bullshit. ARGH-aret was pushing *your* levers and pulling *your* cords as much as you was pushing and pulling hers. You sure didn't see the affair with that attorney coming, did you?

JOE

Too true, Reg. I'm so tired of playing *animal-dummy* games.

MISTER VOX
(voiceover)
Static. It's all static.

REG

Agh! Jesus, that scared the shit out of me!

JOE

As usual, though, Mr. Vox is correct. Aside from their literally sickening, behavioral infections, animal-dummies just have too many unknown levers and cords for even a master ventriloquist like me to find and pull.

REG

Ugh. Who has time for all that?

JOE

Who indeed, Reg? Even nonhuman animals (so like their human counterparts) can be influenced by factors outside of a lone ventriloquist's control. And that lack of control can lead to the *ventriloquist* being manipulated in spite of his best efforts. Dummies dumbly pulling a ventriloquist's cords? Unacceptable.

REG

Yeah! Fuck that! We need to pull up stakes and get the hell outta here.

JOE

Spot on, Reg.

(picking up pen and paper and writing)
STEP 11. "Remove yourself from animal-dummies."
(turning to audience)
Surround yourself with the non-sentient variety.

SCENE 5

(THE FACTORY. JOE sits, slumped and dissipated looking—a once snazzy performer's suit dingy and stained. His hair is longer and unkempt, and he has a short, grizzled beard. REG sits unanimated upon JOE'S knee.)

JOE
(Addressing the audience through the mirror, which now is outlined with the suggestion of light bulbs)

Some time ago, after my animal-dummy lady friend took off with her animal-dummy boss, I moved into this derelict paper mill. It's known simply as "The Factory." I discovered it hidden away in the city's municipal park. I own it now, or I might as well. At Mr. Vox's nocturnal suggestion, I put a few things together and made it happen. This is not the ventriloquist apprentice's concern. Some animal-dummies come and go—a talkative contractor I paid to make some essential repairs to the leaking Factory roof, a surly grocery deliveryman. Even an old homeless rummy who attempts to break into the Factory now and then just to keep me on my toes. They all serve their function and leave. Through means I won't discuss I make enough money to get by in what passes for the outside world. Enough to satisfy my basic needs anyway. Yes, again, these methods often make one very uncomfortable indeed, but we must recall that the road to Greater Ventriloquism is not a simple one. I made this choice, and you made this choice, my pupils: now we must all stick to it! Follow my lead. Listen to your dream-instructor, keep your moral qualms to yourself and toughen up. I once believed my little cottage and my two animal-dummies (the dog and the lady friend) were my life's foundation. How ridiculous. Here I am living in this ramshackle mill house without comfort, without communication contraptions and with little security. Those comforts make you lazy; those devices distract you; that security dulls your senses. And you'll need all your power and concentration to finish the difficult—at times excruciating—work ahead.

> (picking up a battered copy of a homemade book)

Remember STEP 1 in "20 Simple Steps to Ventriloquism?" "How to hold your mouth"? "Always practice in front of a mirror." Any lesser ventriloquist knows that. But I've recently come to appreciate the hidden truth behind this mirror-work for the aspiring Greater Ventriloquist. Reggie, remember when I warned you to stop looking at the mirror if you began to see a kind of black fog in it?

REG
> (coming to life)

What? What? Uh, I think so.

JOE

Well, we're not only ready to stop avoiding this effect—we're ready to exacerbate it for our own purposes.

> (addressing audience)

If you're anything like me, success will bring you and your craft rewards you can't imagine. Yes, our ventriloquist practice has been hindered in a myriad of ways over the years, whether via an overly demanding lady friend or an incessantly ringing phone (or other alarming, infernal communication devices). They distract you from your practice with screeching deadlines. You've never before had the essential components (absence of comfort, distraction and security) that you've needed all this time to move beyond the trivial illusions of lesser ventriloquism into the exciting, at times even startling world of Greater Ventriloquism. At last you're ready.

> (Thick black fog begins filling the stage, spilling out into the auditorium. The huge shadow of MISTER VOX looms behind and above JOE and REG.)

REG

Uh, who the hell are you talking to, Jo-Jo?

JOE

Never mind.
(Back to audience)
You—like me—should now have a more or less isolated and silent (if unsafe) place to work. Yes, you—like me—should now be rid of all non-essential connections to the animal-dummy world and its maddening contraptions. Now there's just you and your dummy and your instructor—your very own Mr. Vox. And your work. Your transition from lesser to Greater Ventriloquism begins now.

REG

Uh, I don't think I wanna learn venkirilikism.

JOE
(ignoring REG)
My own transition began in the Factory's creaking control room situated above the service bins—a rather tall, dilapidated space with walls on three sides. I've installed a large mirror here. It's of the sort favored by actors and their ilk to assist in applying makeup and donning costumes. Of course, any larger than average mirror will do for you and your J.S. ventriloquist doll.

REG

Hey! I ain't no doll! I'm a dummy, dummy!

JOE
(ignoring REG)
As long as the reflection of two more or less human heads (one adult sized, one child sized) sitting side by side can be seen reflected in it. Heed the nocturnal advice of your own master instructor on the particulars. In my case, Mr. Vox led me to this truly rare and excellent room I've just described.
(SOUND: airplane passing over)

Here it's easy to forget the occasional rumbling and roaring of the outside world. Speaking of which, one element that is more of an annoyance than anything is the occasional sound of a low flying plane outside and above this building. No practice space is without its flaws. One special note: whatever mirror you choose for your work should be located in a space almost completely devoid of any natural light. Mr. Vox's choice in my case was superb. There are few architectural structures that can be made more lightless than the control room of a well-constructed paper mill. Of course, you must have some form of light for your work, but it must be quite dim. I favor a tiny lamp bulb wrapped in a dark blue gel of the sort used for dressing backstage between scenes. If procuring this kind of light is beyond your means, you may use a nightlight covered in duct tape. The illumination must be sparse enough so that you can just barely see yourself and your dummy in the mirror. Prepare your space and allow your eyes a few minutes to adjust, giving you and your own J.S. ventriloquist doll time to settle in.

REG

Hello! No dolls here! Only dummies!

JOE
(ignoring REG)

Ventriloquists talk to themselves. It's a fact—an inescapable side effect of all those thousands of practice sessions staring at yourself in a mirror. All those thousands of hours spent manufacturing a pretend relationship with a doll. But Mr. Vox has stripped me of these delusions of dummy-identity. In the words of Mr. Vox himself, *it is a trifle.* And I know it's high time to dispense with these sentimental trappings and get down to real work.

(The animated REG goes slack as JOE tosses the dummy to the ground.)

Which brings us to the inevitable: you are completely on

your own from here on out. It's every ventriloquist for himself I'm afraid. I don't need you anymore. That's right, friend—I'm showing you the door. I doubt you've had the kind of success I've had. And even if you tried to apply the steps to come hundreds, thousands or even millions of times, I'm afraid you would ultimately meet with failure.

(Lifting his battered book up)
Believe me, these twenty simple steps just aren't for you. Besides, I've found I don't care for the idea of competition in the world of Greater Ventriloquism, and I hope for your sake that you never cross my path or my mind in the exciting days to come. Not that you have any more substance or function to me than this dummy. Yes, so long, my pupils. What was to be a guide for the general (if small) aspiring ventriloquist population has now become a self-help book on Greater Ventriloquism. And, of course, by "self" I mean *me*. No more dummies at all.

SCENE 6

(THE FACTORY, some weeks later. JOE sits in front of the mirror in worse shape. Shaggy-headed and filthy. REG remains where JOE tossed him in SCENE 5. The black fog is still thick and MR. VOX's silhouette hulks hugely behind JOE.)

JOE
(JOE's mouth drops open when he speaks and closes when he's silent, but his lips never move when he talks, nor will they again.)

It's mirror-work time. Your name is Joseph Robert Snavely, and you live in the Factory. Hello, handsome. Not looking so great, though, are you? Too much practice; precious little time for personal hygiene.

MR. VOX
A trifle.

JOE
Mr. Vox is right—as usual. You can hardly feel the needle in your neck.

MR. VOX
You had another odd dream last night, didn't you?

JOE
Yes, Mr. Vox.

(The FACTORY set splits apart, revealing the COTTAGE BEDROOM again. REG rises and starts crawling on the ground. MARGARET is lowered from the fly gallery above. JOE and MARGARET and REG go through the motions that MR. VOX describes.)

MR. VOX

You dreamed that you and your ex-lady friend were together again. You were pretending your dummy was a child—*your* child. You were babbling at it and coddling it. *Static.*

JOE

Yes, Mr. Vox.

> (A moving couch enters from upstage with a stuffed dog upon it, and JOE, MARGARET and REG seat themselves. The scene shifts to a racetrack, which resembles the NIGHT AIRPORT outside. Lights flash around the characters, indicating they are traveling speedily along on their moving couch.)

MR. VOX

You seemed to *feel* again without the need for analysis or calculation. In the dream, you and Margaret (yes, beautiful Margaret) and your dummy, Reggie, and that good old, perfectly obedient dog of yours were all riding on a moving couch at stupendous speeds around a racetrack at night. Dear Reg was upon your knee and dear Margaret and dear cur were cuddled up on either side of you on the couch as it moved around at terrific speeds. The racetrack was lit with the fluorescent and sodium blur of stadium lights. Or was it the entrance to an airport?

JOE

I don't know, Mr. Vox.

MR. VOX

The sensation of intense speed made your stomach twist. It kept you pinned in your place as you and the dog and Margaret and Reggie all squealed and laughed in delight.

JOE

(giggling)

Maybe I shouldn't a had that last bottle, cuz I'm feelin' a little plastered.

REG

(head spinning completely backwards to look up at JOE.)

A little *plastered?* More like you had a wax and shine job, dummy boy! Yuk yuk yuk!

MR. VOX

Then the scene shifted to the inside of your snug, little cottage.

(REG is placed down on the floor and JOE and MARGARET silently mimic conversation.)

You began chatting with gorgeous Margaret, who was beaming at you with new respect and—you suspected—a growing physical attraction.

(REG begins trying to pull himself up on his feet.)

After a minute or two of stimulating conversation, you looked up just in time to see Reggie taking its first baby steps—slatted mouth open and big blue, glass eyes shifting back and forth as if with wonder and excitement—stumbling towards you like a one-year-old infant might. And you imagined you felt a great affection towards it, didn't you? You opened your arms to the toddling dummy, and Reggie fell into them and buried its head in your chest. You even felt tears welling in your eyes. But when you looked back at Margaret—a proud grin fixed upon your face—you were surprised that your lady friend's eyes were wide with horror and disbelief.

MARGARET

Oh, holy fuck. You must be making it move with your mind.

JOE

Language.

MR. VOX

...you said. Feeling unperturbed, you looked down at the dummy, holding it out from your body, being careful not to physically touch its controls.

JOE

Let's see if this works.
>   (REG rises into the air and his head begins to
>   spin, slowly at first, and then picking up pace.)

MR. VOX

And you *willed* the dummy's head to spin. And you *willed* its eyes to move. And then you started trying to make the dummy *stop* moving, but you couldn't, could you?

JOE

No, Mr. Vox.
>   (Characters and set change as described
>   below.)

MR. VOX

Its head was spinning around now at an unnatural speed, and its eyes were rolling around with an equal frenzy. And you could feel the little cottage beginning to change as well, windows and walls breathing in and out—floor buckling. And—in an instant—the cottage was gone; the dog was gone; and the dummy was gone. You were in a void containing only you and Margaret, now possessed with obvious panic and horror. As if Margaret was in the midst of its own nightmare and you were the hub of that nightmare. Its left arm was twitching, its head shifting back and forth. And you stared back at your convulsing, crying ex-lady friend—still feeling completely calm and devoid of any emotion you could name.

JOE
(In Mr. Vox's voice)

Who is he?

MR. VOX

...you quietly asked it.
> (The FACTORY set returns, and a filthy
> pallet rises on its foot behind JOE, giving the
> audience a bird's eye view. JOE reclines on it
> and closes his eyes.)

And in the darkness of the Factory machine shop, you could
feel a presence, hulking over you inside the control booth.
(*"What are you?"* Mr. Vox asked.)

JOE
> (eyes clenched closed, JOE writhes.)

I'm... I'm hurting.

MR. VOX

You *imagine* you're hurting. You can't get that dream out of
your head. You imagine you miss your long lost animal-
dummies, don't you? (*"What are you?"* Mr. Vox asked.) You
may well need help. You imagine you miss them, even—
especially—that duplicitous, animal-dummy ex-lady friend of
yours. What was its name?

JOE
> (Eyes open, wide and staring. The pallet falls
> to the ground.)

Margaret.

MR. VOX

Yes, Margaret. (*"What are you?"* Mr. Vox asked.) Why not win
it back? You could easily do that now.

JOE

Yes, Mr. Vox.

> (JOE rises into the air, limbs akimbo, mouth

ajar.)

MR. VOX

Thanks to your tremendous powers of Greater Ventriloquism, you can do almost anything.
(Blackout.)

What are you?

(SOUND: airplane passing over.)

Escape to Thin Mountain

Little Evie is singing again.

It began after we found the body in the train yard. We were making the rounds, looking for stray knickknacks, when we heard a tiny, chiming voice in the wind. It was coming from inside the compartment car of the old *Whippoorwill* express train, which hadn't run for forty years or more. There was a moldy old tent kind of covering up one of the nasty benches. Smelled but not as bad as it must have once. The body, not much more than a skeleton, was holding Little Evie. That shook us all up something awful, even though the corpse face looked so peaceful, happy even.

Then Little Evie began to sing, and we took her as our own.

And now Little Evie is singing again. It's one of her shorter ones—the kind we love, the kind we need. That lilting baby coo voice of hers, the ringing tones so familiar, like reading a diary you wish you had written but deeper, better than that.

Her song this time is an old one about a mountain far away from this close heat, these factories vomiting smoke out all day and night. We know the song so well. It takes place up in the altitudes where a body's head can clear out and take in chilly relief.

> *Crooked trees and reedy light,*
> *Thin stone fingers obscure sight,*
> *Through mazy brush's skeleton,*
> *Creeps the dwarf who shows you in.*

Oh, Little Evie knows where we want to be, and her chiming voice can almost take us there for real and true. She knows what we need.

Little Evie knows we need Thin Mountain.

We'll try to take the train one more time. The train bound for Thin Mountain.

Lord knows we love a good train ride. Always have. Sitting up in that fine old dark wood compartment car watching the smog of the city just fade away into pinewoods, oaks, magnolias standing in a dirt clearing, reaching up untrimmed, like rows and rows of mushroom clouds springing out of the earth. Ugliness returns with every city you reach, the train stations always running in the bad parts of town, but then—

Little Evie is singing again.

She knows how much we love a good train ride, knows where we want, where we need, to go.

Thin Mountain. Not on any map we've ever seen or heard about. Only can be called there. Selected.

Up and up into open country where the wooded trees fall off and those foothills begin stepping up and up, big red and gray rocks like giant-children had stood atop the fingered peaks and pushed them down the side of the mountain to smash and sit forever in petrified silence.

Last time we took the train, oh, it was years back. We were traveling up to Nashville for Little Evie to become a star. We'd been telling everyone about her. That's the place to go if you want to sing and make it stick. Now we didn't do it to take advantage of Little Evie's gift of voice, to make profit from it. We just wanted to share her special gift with everyone like us, wanted to hear Little Evie singing on top of one of those great fingers of rock above so high and clean above the filth of the world below. Wanted to see Little Evie get her due.

That's the day we all first heard the name Thin Mountain, the day the man said it at the train station just before he threw himself in front of the *Whippoorwill* Express train, got cut in two but with that look of healing joy on his face.

And never did Little Evie sing so beautifully than she did as we rumbled, rocking back and forth, up north towards Thin Mountain.

Crooked trees and reedy light,
Thin stone fingers obscure sight,
Through mazy brush's skeleton,
Creeps the dwarf who shows you in.

She sang so everyone in the compartment car could hear and see and feel the things she was singing about. Their heads, bald or styled or messy, turned, swiveled to listen to Little Evie croon. We knew at that moment that Thin Mountain must be real because every word that Little Evie sang that day came true in front of our eyes. We saw those fingerlike peaks and the lovely, crooked trees so old and wise looking below them. A friendly *Wizard of Oz* kind of dwarf grinned at us through the glass of the train car as Little Evie's voice chimed in our ears. We were so close to Thin Mountain—we felt like we all were at that moment. A place for us to be.

Thin Mountain, Thin Mountain, Thin Mountain—

Then we had a bad dream, just like the ones we sometimes get. A policeman, that fat one we like, was pulling us down from the car, always so gentle that one, past the ruined seats, out of the train. Told us Thin Mountain wasn't real. And then we were back where we started, somehow, in Municipal Park next to the old train engine. Little Evie had stopped singing. She was scared, and we gave that nice, fat policeman a good tongue thrashing and then felt bad for it. We scuttled back down underneath the highway overpass again and under the big cardboard box house. It gets cold during the paper mill days, and we cough a lot, though Little Evie doesn't ever seem to care. We start thinking the gentle, big-bellied policeman pulling us off our train, even the train ride itself was part of the dream. We get confused sometimes. Little Evie won't sing about it and sometimes we think maybe it didn't happen at all.

We remember her song about Thin Mountain, though. Little Evie's song—like the one she's singing now—was all made up, spur of the moment like, never to return or be duplicated, melting away like one of those fancy ice sculptures you see sometimes. Those are special songs of hers, songs we try to sing ourselves from memory, but we always get the words messed up, and those ringing notes Little Evie can hit we doubt anyone else can, let alone any of us. No one can sing like her.

Little Evie gets real sad sometimes. She says her life is low and the light in the morning coming down through the interstate slats hurts her head. So much so that she doesn't want to eat or even sleep some days. We hate those times because she never even sings, sometimes for so long, and when she doesn't sing, we all get sad and become a sight to anyone passing by in their cars or the bus and sometimes even bicycles. They help us sometimes, feeling sorry, and we see the inside of the hospital rooms for a while, which Little Evie doesn't like and then if she sings there it's a hate kind of singing that makes the hospital people think their teeth are falling out or makes them feel her tiny voice is an insect-thing drilling into their brains. Little Evie can be real mean when she doesn't care about anything.

Then again, sometimes Little Evie gets agitated like our own mama used to get so often. Like we can get too. It runs in the family maybe. Those times Little Evie kind of talk-sings fast, so fast we can't understand the words or follow the crazy melodies, and it makes her mad when we don't understand or like her songs. And that makes us upset—our hearts beating so fast we're afraid we'll choke and stop breathing.

Sometimes we get real sick, and Little Evie starts feeling feverish to our hands (when she'll let us touch her). She tells us to leave, that nothing and no one can help her. She won't stop moving, can't sleep, can't find a moment's peace. Then it seems like Thin Mountain is so far away and like nothing and nobody will speak or even look at us again. No one stops by our cardboard house under the overpass to give us a dollar, a nickel, even one penny at times like that.

And then Little Evie disappears altogether. Those are the worst times for us. We can't reach her or hear her voice, and then she is all we can think about all day long, walking along the little park roads with our bags full of special knickknacks that Little Evie found for us once in a dumpster outside of the Indoor Swamp. We camp out in the park, swinging on the swings that Little Evie used to like so much back when she liked much of anything, watching the pushy squirrels beg for food. They made her laugh when she used to laugh. And then suddenly—

Little Evie is singing again.

Just when it seems everything is on the verge of just staying sad or upset or like nothing at all, Little Evie starts singing for us. And then everything is alright for a while.

> *Crooked trees and reedy light,*
> *Thin stone fingers obscure sight,*
> *Through mazy brush's skeleton,*
> *Creeps the dwarf who shows you in.*

We've been all getting headaches lately, and Little Evie cries at night from it sometimes. She hates it here. We wonder if she ever liked it, if she ever likes us, at all. She understands us better than anyone does. We love her, and not just her singing. We are lost without her, and it hurts when those other voices tell us she doesn't like us, doesn't love us... maybe even hates us. And then we try to sing to her.

> *We pray We pray We pray*
> *That Little Evie will never go away.*

Not long back we woke up and saw what looked like Little Evie standing on the concrete teeth-fence thing on either side of the interstate above our cardboard house. We thought she was singing or crying in the rain. We were scared Little Evie would jump.

But when we ran so fast up the side of the entrance ramp and got up there to save her, trying not to slip and break our legs or maybe even our necks while we did it, it wasn't Little Evie up there at all. Instead there was a dwarf, that grinning dwarf we saw through the window that time on the train to Thin Mountain, that time we were maybe dreaming, and he wasn't singing like Little Evie either, but he was dancing, just kind of a herky-jerky dance on those crazy bowlegs with big flat feet, and he was laughing real low while he did it, thrusting out his tongue and those little hips in a kind of way that made us feel bad and shamed like.

We were drenched in the rain watching him, wanting to climb back down but wondering where Little Evie was and wondering if this dwarf had maybe done something to her something bad or something shameful, and so we climbed up with the intent to grab and squeeze and demand and there were cars and jeeps and buses and such honking and heads screaming out bad words. Once we made it to the top, we tried to get a look at the hateful little man but he wasn't there at all, it was only ever us up there, and we were looking down down to the pavement below, real dizzy like, and it maybe seemed like Thin Mountain was down there, as if the pavement was a chalk drawing you could jump into like in *Mary Poppins* or maybe if we jumped the world would flip upside down and we'd find ourselves floating up like a feather, maybe all the way to Thin Mountain and wouldn't that be nice.

We don't know how we got back down inside our waterlogged box (it's almost time to find another one), but—

Little Evie is singing again. She's singing, but she's not really here either. We can't see her or feel her little hand in ours. Little Evie's voice seems like the only thing left of her.

She's been singing for so long now, but it's a different kind of song than we've heard before. It's soft like rabbit fur and sometimes sounds kind of inside-out too, maybe broken headed hospital-words like jumping off the interstate overpass and finding yourself on the top of a mountain. It's the kind of half singing-half talking Little Evie does sometimes that you can't understand, but it doesn't stop.

It's the kind of singing that makes us cry, not all sad kind of crying but mixed in with the sweet kind of crying, like remembering the dusky smell of a childhood friend who is gone gone passed forever now but still somehow with us at that moment. A friend who would never leave us, who loved us once but doesn't anymore, and did leave at last and is gone gone passed forever now and yet is still haunted-house here somehow.

But Little Evie keeps singing and the sweet crying turns into something else, more like mad crying or throw up crying, like where are we why are we kill us kill kill us crying. And at that moment it seems like the concrete is bad quicksand gobbling up cars, buses, tilting buildings, and the paper mill days hide monsters we can never see only smell and the interstate overpass is draining or melting bit by bit and the molten looking asphalt and concrete of it will cover us and draw us down so far away from the thick air under the interstate overpass let alone the thin, cold air of Thin Mountain, and Little Evie is singing so loud and it is everything and it is too much.

And Little Evie keeps singing.

Now. Making our way, stumbling, falling, wheeling up the interstate ramp, a sight a sight a sight on the shoulder under the sun that can't be seen through all the brown smoke trying to avoid the fog beasts and throw up skeletons and pavement quicksand all day long till we finally reach downtown and the train station and the train yard and we're crying and screaming and howling, trying to drown out Little Evie's song that we don't want to feel anymore that we don't want to be anymore. But it never ends, on endless loop like, and we love Little Evie so much we only ever wanted her to be happy healthy, but we know that this can't be down here in smogtown, no it's not possible down here with the church gargoyles staring, tongues out nasty like, eyes rolling, smog fat people grinning black eyed from their patrol cars at us.

And, all at once, there's the old *Whippoorwill* express train, which hasn't run for forty years or more, but is standing in the sudden sunlight gleaming black and new and polished and green, and a big-bellied dwarf-conductor is smiling at us not mean or nasty at all but friendly and funny, and he does a herky-jerky welcome jig as he takes our ticket, and we are all young, and it is quiet except for the shhhhh of the steam engine as it prepares for the journey ahead. We make our way through the train cars, and as we do, we can hear the singing.

The sound of Little Evie's voice chimes in the air, cold and clear, makes us see and feel those deeply familiar things as only she can. And now I understand the words. Puppets dangling in a quiet void, their eyes rolling. Giant crab arm crooking out of fog. Whole worlds of quivering things and silent, broken things and colors so thick with light that they become a kaleidoscope of darkness. Mazes of screaming mirrors. Dreadful things. Wonderful things.

We enter the train's fancy but cramped bathroom in the dining car and look into the mirror to smile at ourselves, not minding the spreading, black crack that appears from our hairline down to our jawline on the other side of our face. One bulb sputters and throbs to Little Evie's voice. We can hear her, feel her, so close now, in the flesh (or what passes for it). Of course, she was waiting for us, calling for us, all this time. Pulling us on towards Thin Mountain with a song like no other.

We enter the empty compartment car, dark wood gleaming.

Dark curtains and carpets, and a kind of tent covering one of the benches furthest from us. We walk towards the tented bench. Towards the singing. Towards little Evie.

"All aboard!" we hear the dwarf-conductor bellow through the window. The tent is closed and a thrill goes through the train cars as we reach to open it.

We can hear Little Evie. She's inside.

> *Crooked trees and reedy light,*
> *Thin stone fingers obscure sight,*
> *Through mazy brush's skeleton,*
> *Creeps the dwarf who shows you in.*
> *Thin Mountain, Thin Mountain, Thin Mountain—*

Shhhhh.
Shhhhh.
Shhhhh.

Little Evie is singing again.

NOTES

(17) Inspired and informed by Bodhipaksa's *Mindfulness of Breathing*.

(21) "Murmurs of a Voice Foreknown" is a phrase from Clark Ashton Smith's poem, "Warning."

(41) The "wise man" quote is paraphrased from *A Course in Miracles*, "Lesson 5."

(53) Donora, PA—the site of the terrible Smog of 1948—had a city limits sign that read "Donora. Next to Yours the Best Town in the U.S.A "

(57) When I was a child, my first ventriloquist dummy came with a pamphlet entitled "7 SIMPLE STEPS TO VENTRILOQUISM." Though the following ventriloquist story went through a tremendous number of transmutations from its inception two decades ago (when it was first conceived), that pamphlet from my past proved to be the key to what "20 Simple Steps to Ventriloquism" would finally become. Practice the first seven steps enough, and you may one day be able to throw your voice with the best of the showbiz ventriloquists out there. Practice the rest of the steps at your own risk.

(99) "The Infusorium" owes a debt to Devra Davis' *When Smoke Ran Like Water: Tales of Environmental Deception And The Battle Against Pollution* and Berton Roueché's *New Yorker* article, "The Fog," both of which educated me on the horrors of pollutants and their immediate and ongoing effects on biological life forms. Kroth's mottled-green, steel oxygen tanks and the term "non-killed" had their origin in anecdotes related to the terrible Donora Smog of 1948, in which "a heavy fog blanketed [the] valley, and as the days passed, the fog became a thick, acrid smog that left about 20 people dead and thousands ill. Not until October 31 did the Donora Zinc Works shut down its furnaces-just hours before rain finally dispersed the smog."

(137) All guru quote excerpts are from a variety of Eckhart Tolle sources. Tolle's philosophy had a tremendous influence on the collection as a whole.

(185) Written after "Ten Steps to Thin Mountain," by Thomas Ligotti—a piece that inspired the first story I didn't throw away, "20 Simple Steps to Ventriloquism."

ACKNOWLEDGMENTS

Various incarnations of these stories first appeared in the following publications:

The Grimscribe's Puppets (Miskatonic River Press, 2013): "20 Simple Steps to Ventriloquism"

Lovecraft eZine: "The Secret of Ventriloquism"

Pseudopod: "20 Simple Steps to Ventriloquism," "Murmurs of a Voice Foreknown," and "The Mindfulness of Horror Practice"

Xnoybis: "The Indoor Swamp"

"The Infusorium" was published in chapbook form (Dunhams Manor Press, 2015)

My gratitude to Jordan Krall for publishing and championing my work, Dave Felton for his artistic wizardry, Anna Trueman for her excellent, elegant design, and Matt Cardin for decades of support, inspiration and friendship.

Thanks to my friends and readers: Patrick Boyton, Brendon Mroz, and Christopher Slatsky.

Special thanks to Shawn Mann and James DeWitt for years of tremendous encouragement, to my parents, Don and Ann Padgett, for their unending support, to my sister, Deborah Padgett, for turning me into a reader, to my spouse, Carolyn Hembree, for her brilliant (and sometimes harrowing) notes, to my daughter, Mamie, for existing and forever lighting the way, and to my friend and mentor, Thomas Ligotti, without whom this book would not exist.

ABOUT THE AUTHOR

Jon Padgett is a professional—though lapsed—ventriloquist who lives in New Orleans with his spouse, their daughter and two cats.

Padgett is a Senior Editor of *Vastarien*: a source of critical study and creative response to the corpus of Thomas Ligotti.

He has work out or forthcoming in *Pseudopod*, *Lovecraft eZine*, *Xnoybis*, *Antenna::Signals* and *The Junk Merchants: A Literary Salute to William S. Burroughs*.

Printed in Great Britain
by Amazon